Toby has known little more than loneliness since he was taken from his home and his family was killed. He's a prisoner, forced to heal the members of the gang that bought him from the men who kidnapped him.

Until he's not.

Camden didn't expect to find out that Sam's brother, the brother who was sold to a gang, is his mate. He's not sure where to go from here. Toby is understandably wary and cautious, and most of the time, he won't let Camden close enough to talk to him. Camden doesn't have a problem giving him the time and space he needs, but they might not have much of it.

When the envoy from another pack arrives and demands Camden give up one of the unicorn shifters, Camden refuses, even though he knows the Rosewood pack doesn't stand a chance. The pack is small, and its members aren't warriors. He's not about to give Toby or Sam up, but he has no idea how his people are going to deal with this — or if they'll make it out alive.

For a Unicorn's Happiness
Copyright © 2019 Catherine Lievens
ISBN: 978-1-4874-2626-2
Cover art by Angela Waters

Published by eXtasy Books Inc or
Devine Destinies, an imprint of eXtasy Books Inc

Look for us online at:
www.eXtasybooks.com or www.devinedestinies.com

For a Unicorn's Happiness
Legendary Shifters Book 2

By

Catherine Lievens

CHAPTER ONE

Toby knew something was wrong before Roy burst into his bedroom looking like he was about to kill someone as painfully as possible.

"Stay in here," he barked.

Toby knew better than to answer, but he needed to know if he was in danger. The last time this had happened, he'd almost been kidnapped, and he wasn't looking forward to going through something like that again. "What's going on?"

"We're under attack."

Toby had suspected that. "Who?"

"Why the fuck does it matter? You better be here when it's over. We're gonna need you."

Toby nodded, but Roy was already out the door. Toby heard the sound of the lock engaging in the door. He sighed and wondered what gang was after him this time. Ever since they'd found out this gang had him, they'd been trying to raid the house every few months, with varying results.

Toby couldn't say he liked being with the bears, but he also knew they were better than a lot of the other gangs. They'd taken him because of what he could do, and that meant that while they didn't have a problem insulting him and scaring him, they also didn't hurt him or touch him in any way. He wouldn't be that lucky with others, as Roy made sure to remind him every so often. He didn't need to—Toby wasn't even thinking about escaping, not anymore.

He had no idea what he'd do if he managed to sneak out. His family was gone. He didn't have friends. He couldn't

1

drive. He was alone in the world and had nowhere to go, and Roy was right. If people found out he was a unicorn shifter and that he could heal with his hands, they'd tear each other apart over him. They already did, although he didn't feel guilty that drug dealers and killers were bleeding and killing each other. There would be fewer bad guys alive by the end of the night.

Roy grabbed Toby's hand and pushed him toward the closet. Toby yelped at a sudden pain in his ankle when he fell to the floor.

"Fuck," Roy growled. "Get in there."

"My ankle—"

"You're not gonna need it. Hide in the closet and make sure to stay there. Don't open the fucking door for anyone but me, got it?"

"Yes."

"I hope for your sake we win this."

Toby hoped that too. He scrambled into the closet, and Roy slammed the door shut behind him. Toby's ankle pulsed, and he was pretty sure he'd twisted it when Roy had pushed him. He didn't think Roy had done it on purpose—although he wouldn't put it past the guy—but this would complicate things if he had to run.

He'd been lucky the other times, but he was always ready. He needed to be.

These were the times when he missed his brother the most. Sam hadn't been that much older than him, but he was his big brother, and he'd always protected Toby.

Until that night.

Thinking about it made it hard to breathe. The people who'd grabbed him had been overjoyed to tell him they'd killed the rest of his family and that they'd mutilated their bodies to get their horns. They'd wanted Toby to be meek and not to fight them, and it had worked. Toby had been in shock, and he barely remembered the first few months after that. He'd been sold a few times until he'd ended up in the hands of this gang, and he'd been with them ever since.

From the sound of it, it looked like that might not last, though.

Toby had been through this already, but he didn't think the yells and screams had ever come that close to his bedroom. He could hear them as if they were right outside, and maybe they were. The bears' luck had to break sooner or later. Maybe today was that day.

Something crashed against the door of his bedroom, and Toby jumped. He tried to crawl deeper into the closet, but there wasn't much space. This was it, in more ways than one. It was the end of the closet, and possibly, the end of Toby's time with the bears.

He wasn't sure how he felt about that. He didn't particularly like the bears, but he realized he'd been lucky to end up with them. He might not be as lucky with the next people he'd be with, and that was the terrifying part of this.

Gunshots made Toby jerk. He swallowed and pressed his back harder against the wall, wondering if pulling down his clothes to cover himself would help. Probably not, since he suspected the people attacking were shifters. They always were, and they'd be able to smell him and to hear him even if he tried to hide.

The bedroom door opened, and footsteps came closer. Toby held his breath and resisted the urge to screw his eyes shut. If he was going to be taken again, he wanted to see everything. He'd closed his eyes the last time, and he'd missed having one last sight of his parents. Closing his eyes also made things confusing, since he couldn't see what was happening, and he needed to be ready in case he had a chance to run. He wasn't sure how he'd manage, but he could always shift if he needed to. Not the best way to be discreet, but at this point, he doubted discretion would help him.

"Anything?" a man asked.

"No," another one answered. "I think this is his room, though."

"It does smell familiar. Could the gang have moved him? Maybe they found out we were coming."

"How could they have? Only people from the pack knew. No, I think he's still here."

"We need to find him then."

"We will. Stand guard at the door. I don't want to be surprised."

"You think he's in here?"

"I don't know, but I'm going to look."

And he was going to find Toby. There was no way he wouldn't.

Toby looked around the closet for something to defend himself with, but there wasn't much. He got up, because he didn't want to be on his ass when the door opened, and he grabbed one of the hangers. It was made of wood, so it was better than nothing, even though it wouldn't do much. The guys out there hadn't sounded angry, but what did Toby know?

He listened as one of the men left the room. The other one stayed right there, though, and Toby suspected he'd made a sound when he'd grabbed the hanger, because the footsteps that came next made a beeline for the closet.

He held his breath again. The man knew exactly where he was, so it was a question of seconds. Toby knew he wouldn't be able to run, not while they were inside the house, but he hoped he could once they left. There were a few houses close to this one, and maybe he could manage to get to one of them and knock. If someone opened, he might be safe.

The closet door creaked open. Toby attacked before he could think better of it, swinging the hanger at the man's head and praying it hit the target.

It didn't.

The man made a surprised noise and ducked.

Toby's thrust missed, and the momentum pushed him forward—straight into the arms of the man, who rose and grabbed him.

They were close—too close.

Toby pushed away, panic rising in his throat. "Let me go!"

The man raised his hands. He was pale, and his eyes were wide, but that didn't stop Toby from noticing how good-looking he was. He was taller than Toby, with wide shoulders and thick arms. Toby couldn't seem to ignore the sensation of having them around him. It made his skin tingle in a way he didn't think he'd ever felt.

The man also had short, blond hair, brown eyes, and was tentatively smiling, which was perhaps even more confusing. "Toby?"

Toby blinked. "You know my name."

"I do. Are you okay?"

Toby held up the hanger. "What do you want?"

"We're here to free you."

That wasn't what Toby had expected to hear, and he wasn't sure how to answer. "Free me?" It couldn't be right. Could it? No one knew he was there. No one out in the world knew him or worried about him.

So why was this man here to free him?

Camden desperately wanted to pull Toby into his arms and take a deep breath. He needed to make sure of what he'd smelled, and for that, he needed Toby closer. That wasn't going to be easy, though. Toby was understandably afraid, and Camden didn't know if mentioning his brother would help. It was the only thing he could think of, though. They needed to hurry. The pack might be winning the fight against the gang, but the police were bound to arrive eventually, and that was one thing Camden wasn't looking forward to.

He kept his hands raised so Toby could see them and hopefully understand he wasn't going to reach for him. "My name is Camden. I'm the alpha of the pack based in Rosewood."

Toby frowned. "Rosewood. That's where I grew up."

"I know. In the woods, with your parents and your brother."

"How do you know that?"

"I've met your brother, Sam."

Toby jerked back. "That's not possible. Sam is dead. They're all dead."

"Sam isn't, I promise. He's waiting for you outside." Toby didn't seem to believe Camden, and Camden wasn't sure how to convince him. "He's a pack member now. One of my friends is his mate, and while they're not bonded yet, they live together."

"Sam is dead," Toby repeated.

His tone broke Camden's heart a little. He could only imagine what Toby had been through, and he hurt for him. He wanted to fix things, but he couldn't, not all of them. "I promise you, he's not, and he's outside. You're a unicorn shifter. You can tell if I'm good of heart, right?"

Toby's eyes narrowed. "How do you know that?"

"Because Sam told me. Read me, Toby. I swear to you that I won't hurt you." Camden wanted to tell him to come closer and smell him, to confirm they were mates, but he wasn't sure if that would freak him out even more, and they needed to leave as soon as possible.

Toby wrinkled his nose. Camden wasn't sure he was reading him or not. He had no idea what that looked like. But then Toby nodded, and Camden saw him relax. He believed him.

"You don't want to hurt me," Toby said.

"I don't."

"I'm still not sure I can trust you."

"I understand that. My goal isn't to use your power as a healer, or the one you used to ascertain I'm good of heart. I don't think I can convince you unless you leave this closet, though, and I don't want to leave you here."

"What about the gang that owns me?"

Suddenly, Camden wanted to get back out there and find the people who thought they *owned* Toby. "No one owns you, even if they paid money for you. You're a human being. You're free."

"That's not what I asked."

"You're right. Sorry. My pack is taking care of them, but this was a rescue mission, so there aren't many of us here. It would be best if we could leave as soon as you feel up to it."

Toby nodded. "All right. I'll come with you." He took a step forward, and his leg buckled.

Camden rushed toward him and grabbed him. "What's wrong?"

"I hurt my ankle earlier. It's nothing bad, I don't think, but it hurts when I walk."

"I can carry you." Now that Toby was in Camden's arms again, Camden was sure of what he'd smelled earlier. Toby was his mate, and the thought was both overwhelming and joyful. Camden had been jealous when Frederic had told him about Sam, even though he'd known that finding his mate would create problems with his mother. He'd known his mate would be a man, and she was pushing for him to get married and have heirs, something Toby wouldn't be able to provide.

But none of that mattered now.

Toby hesitated. He obviously still wasn't sure he could trust Camden, and that was okay. Camden gave him time to think because he needed it. If someone came in, Camden would deal with them.

Toby finally nodded. "All right. You can carry me."

Camden let out a relieved sigh. "Is there anything you need to take from this room?"

"All of this is stuff the gang bought for me. You can set it on fire if you want."

There was fire in Toby, even though the gang had no doubt tried to beat it out of him. "I'm going to lean down and put one arm around your back and another under your knees. Okay?"

Toby nodded. He dropped the hanger he'd still been holding and leaned closer to Camden. Camden reached for him, hooking his arms around him where he'd said he would, and hauled him up.

Toby was light, too light. "Did they feed you?" Camden asked with a grunt. The idea of Toby being unfed and mistreated made him want to hurt someone, possibly the people who'd done that to him.

"Most of the time," Toby said as if it were perfectly normal not to give people food.

"Most of the time?" Camden asked with a growl.

To his surprise, Toby patted his chest and snuggled closer. "I like that you're all indignant on my account, but you don't need to be. Those guys weren't exactly good, you know. They dealt drugs, trafficked people, those kinds of things. I'm lucky they gave me food and slapped me around only a few times."

"They hurt you?"

"It was only a few slaps, I promise."

That was too much for Camden's taste, but he knew his anger wouldn't change anything. He carried Toby out of the bedroom and nodded at Griffin. Griffin took a step closer, but Camden shook his head. He hoped his beta would understand he needed to stay away for now. The last thing they needed was for Toby to get spooked and decide he didn't trust Camden anymore.

Camden wasn't sure how he'd deal with that. He *wanted* Toby to trust him. He wasn't sure why Toby hadn't yet said anything about them being mates, but he had to know, since his face was pressed against the side of Camden's neck.

It was both heaven and hell. Camden wanted to do much more than hold Toby, but he couldn't, no matter who Toby was to him, no matter what he smelled like. Pushing too hard too fast would only scare Toby, and Camden couldn't allow anyone to do that, not even himself.

"Where is everyone?" Camden asked Griffin as they walked along the hallway. The house was fucking huge, and it had taken them too long to find Toby, who'd been in one of the smallest and plainest bedrooms.

"I haven't heard from Rowan yet, but Reece and the others are good."

"Should we worry about Rowan?"

"Probably not."

They didn't, because he was waiting by the front door with Reece. He grinned like a loon and gestured out the door. "Ready?"

Something exploded behind them, shaking the house. Camden swore and followed Reece and Rowan outside, shielding Toby with his body.

"What the fuck was that?" he asked as they ran.

"I had a little fun in their kitchen," Rowan answered. "And by kitchen, I mean the one where they produced drugs."

Camden rolled his eyes. "Is the house going to be standing by the time this is over?"

"Yeah, of course. I made sure the stuff got destroyed, but not the house. It'll make a nice place for a new family once it gets sold, don't you think?"

"It would have to be a big family."

"So? Even big families need a place to live."

Camden stopped listening to him and headed toward the

spot where he'd left the others earlier. He knew Sam was probably dying to get to Toby, and while Camden didn't want to relinquish the hold he had on his mate, this was more important. He'd have time later to talk to Toby and ask him what he thought, what he wanted from their bond. Toby had been convinced that Sam was dead, though, and Camden wanted to give him this.

He noticed Sam standing there with Frederic and noticed the exact moment Sam realized that the man Camden was carrying was his brother. Camden had to tense to avoid getting bowled over when Sam slammed into them and wrapped himself around Toby—and Camden, since he was still holding his mate.

Toby squeaked when something slammed against him and Camden. He tried to press closer to Camden than he already was, but that wasn't possible, since he was in Camden's arms, so he tried to push away. Maybe if he could jump out of Camden's hold, he could defend himself from whoever this was.

He turned to try, and his heart stopped. He sucked in a breath, and he wasn't sure if he let it out again. He wasn't sure he was still breathing, not with Sam standing there, apparently trying to crawl into Camden's arms to get to Toby.

Toby let go of Camden and wrapped his arms around his brother, yelling, "Sam!" He couldn't believe this. He couldn't believe Sam was still alive, not after he'd thought he was dead for so long.

Why had he believed the people who'd told him that? Why had he let them convince him that he was alone in the world?

Camden wiggled as if trying to get away, but he was stuck, wrapped around Toby and Sam as much as they were wrapped around him. He gave up after a moment, moving toward a man who was waiting for them further down the sidewalk. He said something about Toby needing rest, but Toby was focused on his brother and didn't listen, not until Sam gently extricated himself from Toby's arms.

He didn't go far, though, grabbing one of Toby's hands and walking with Camden as he headed toward a truck parked close by. Toby wasn't afraid anymore. Sam was alive, and he wouldn't be with people he didn't trust and who weren't good.

Camden hadn't been lying, thank God. Toby wasn't sure what he would have done if he'd had to deal with the fact that his mate was a bad man.

Toby couldn't stop smiling. He let Camden help him into the back seat of the truck, and he and Sam had to let go, but Sam rushed around the truck so he could sit next to Toby. They reached for each other and hugged again now that they were more comfortable and that Camden wasn't stuck between them anymore.

"God, I didn't think I'd ever see you again," Sam murmured against Toby's neck.

Toby swallowed. It wasn't an easy thing to do around the knot in his throat. "Same. I thought I'd have to spend the rest of my life in this place." Unless another gang had managed to get to him, and he'd always known that wouldn't be a good thing. "I can't believe you're here. How did you find me? How did you escape when the men came to take us? Where have you been all this time?" Toby had so many questions and so few answers. He wanted to know everything. He wanted to know if Sam had been alone or if he's been with the pack.

Sam leaned back. He looked pale, although that might only be because Toby hadn't seen him in so long. "Mom told me to run. I hid in the forest."

Toby remembered hearing their mom screaming that. He hadn't managed to get to the back door in time, but he was relieved to know that Sam had, that at least he had gotten away. "Please tell me you had help to deal with them after." Sam might be alive, but Toby knew their parents weren't. He'd seen the blood on those men's hands. He'd seen the horns they'd stolen. He hadn't seen their bodies, but he knew they'd been there, and he hated thinking about Sam having to face the aftermath alone.

Sam shook his head. "I've been living in the forest since then."

Toby's throat closed, and he looked Sam in the eyes. Sam was crying, and Toby wasn't far from doing the same thing, but he needed to take care of his brother.

He dried the tears on Sam's cheek. "Sammy. God, I hate that you had to go through this on your own." He forced himself to smile. "But you're not alone anymore, are you?" Toby hadn't missed what Camden had said about Sam having met his mate. He hadn't believed it, but now he did—he'd seen a man who'd been hovering by Sam when Toby and Camden had left the gang's house.

Sam shook his head. His smile was tremulous, but it was there. "No. I met my mate."

Toby felt his smile widen without him thinking about it. This news made him happy. "Yeah? And he's a member of that pack who lived near us?" Camden might have said so, but Toby had a bit of trouble remembering most things that had been said in the past fifteen minutes.

"He is."

"That's great. So is my mate." Toby felt better now that he could say that to someone. He wanted to laugh and smile and be *happy*. He hadn't felt this giddy since his parents had been alive.

Sam blinked. "Your mate?"

Toby could tell what Sam thought even though Sam didn't add anything. He could still read his brother as well as he had when they were younger. He looked toward the front of the truck. He could see Camden standing there, talking to who he presumed was Sam's mate and another two men. They kept looking toward the house, but Toby couldn't tell whether they were worried, not when it was so dark. "Yes. He said his name is Camden."

Sam's eyes went even wider. "*Camden* is your mate?"

"Yes, or at least I'm pretty sure he is. He smells like my mate." That was one of the reasons Toby hadn't fought him as much as he would have any other man when the closet door had opened.

"I can't believe it."

Toby frowned. Sam didn't sound unhappy at the news, but his reaction wasn't what Toby had expected. "Why not? He seems like a good man, and you know him better than me."

"Oh, that's not it. I'm happy for you both, and he *is* a good man. He's also the pack's alpha, though."

Toby blinked. Had Camden told him that? Had Toby missed it through the fear and confusion? It wasn't something one wouldn't mention, but the situation hadn't been ideal. Hell, he and Camden hadn't even talked about the fact that they were mates.

"Hey," Sam said, taking Toby's hand. "The fact that Camden is the alpha doesn't change anything. He's a good man. He accepted me in the pack without a problem and defended me from the men who killed our parents. He helped me make sure they paid for what they did."

"He killed them?" Toby wasn't sure he disliked that thought, even though he knew he should.

Sam's cheeks flushed. "Let's just say that not all of them are in a good state, and it's not all due to Camden."

"You fought them?" Sam had always been a sweet, gentle boy, then man. Toby had a hard time imagining him killing anyone.

"Not exactly. I did promise one of them I'd heal him if he

told me where you were, though. I didn't, not even when he admitted selling you to this gang. That was this morning. I'm not sure I've processed everything yet, to be honest. I don't want you to think I'm a monster, though."

"I don't. I could never think that." Toby realized he and Sam weren't the kids they'd been before their parents had been killed.

Toby had spent years in the hands of the gang, healing them when they were wounded and being treated like nothing more than a commodity. Sam had been alone all that time. He'd lived in the woods, and he'd had to take care of their parents' bodies. Even though he had a new family now, and a mate, what had happened had left its traces, on both of them. They were going to have to relearn who they were and how to be brothers, but Toby didn't mind. It was certainly better than being in the gang's house and catering to them.

They had time now. Toby was free, and Sam was home. Toby didn't know what was going to happen, but that was okay. He wasn't afraid, not when he had Sam, and maybe Camden. He was safe, and he had time to figure things out.

Camden was angry. Now that he wasn't worried about finding Toby and getting him out of that house, everything he'd seen and everything Toby had told him was crowding his mind.

The gang had used him. They'd abused him, maybe not physically, but mentally. They'd slapped him around like Toby had said, and the thought made Camden want to go back inside and strangle the people still standing.

"You look like you want to tear someone's head off," Frederic said. "Was it that bad?"

Camden swallowed. The last thing he wanted was to scare Toby, or anyone else. He was the alpha, and he couldn't let emotions rule him. "The important part is that he's okay."

"Yeah, but it's probably a good idea to know what we're looking forward to."

Camden sighed and rubbed his face. "He's my mate." And that complicated everything.

Frederic blinked. "Yeah? We managed to score two brothers?"

Camden loved him for not mentioning they were both unicorn shifters. Unicorns, and other kinds of rare shifters, were sought out, used, and abused because of what they were. Camden couldn't have cared less about what Toby was, but he couldn't deny that his being a unicorn wouldn't make things easy, for either of them or the pack.

Having two unicorns was unheard of. Usually, as soon as people found out about a unicorn family, they tore them apart, just like what had happened to Sam and Toby. Unicorns were too valuable not to use, and Camden didn't like that people still thought that way. He couldn't do anything to change it, though. He *would* do everything he could to protect Sam and Toby, but he knew it wasn't going to be easy.

"You don't look happy, or at least, not as happy as you ought to be," Frederic pointed out.

"I'm worried, mostly. You know what's going to happen when this gets out."

Frederic's smile faded. "Yeah. You're not going to let anyone hurt them, though."

"I'm not, but that doesn't mean they won't be hurt. I'll do what I can, but the pack is small, and we don't have that many fighters."

Frederic patted Camden's shoulder. "Why don't we think about that later? We should take them home. Unless you want to wait around for the police to arrive? I'm surprised they're not here yet, with all the noise and the small explosion."

"That was Rowan, but yeah. I'll ask Griffin to call them

once we're on the road."

Frederic nodded. "Get some rest once we're there. I know things aren't going to be easy, but you won't solve anything by obsessing over it right now. Let's get past tonight first. We'll think about the rest tomorrow. Besides, you found your mate. You should give yourself a moment to celebrate that and to enjoy the feeling."

Frederic wasn't wrong. Camden hadn't let himself savor the moment, because he'd been worried about getting Toby out of the house and back to his brother. He could use some time to wrap his mind around meeting Toby and what it would mean.

"Let me see if Griffin managed to find everyone. Then we'll be out of here."

Frederic grinned. "I'll drive. I suspect you'll be too distracted to keep your eyes on the road."

"Possibly." Camden's chest felt like it might burst with everything he was feeling. He couldn't make heads or tails of anything right now except for the fact that he'd found Toby and Toby was his mate. He had no idea what it meant for the future, but he'd find out soon enough.

His mother was going to be pissed. She wanted him to have heirs because she still thought being an alpha should be a hereditary charge. That was how Camden had become an alpha, but if he'd had a choice, he'd have turned it down. He *hadn't* had a choice, though, and he'd found himself in charge of people's lives at only twenty-eight.

And now he wouldn't be giving his mother an heir, at least not the way she wanted him to. Yeah, she was going to go nuclear, and it wasn't something Camden wanted to subject Toby to. Toby didn't deserve to feel like he wasn't welcome when he was—even if not by Camden's mother. Hopefully, she'd accept him in time. Camden wasn't going to cast Toby aside because he couldn't give him children. He wouldn't have even if Toby hadn't been his mate and he'd just been in love with him.

He climbed into the passenger side after making sure everyone who'd come with them was accounted for. Griffin was going to make the phone call to the police to make sure the gang members they'd left behind were arrested. Humans tended to stay away from shifters when they could, but they'd have a hard time ignoring the drugs and everything else in the house. Even they couldn't close an eye and wait for other shifters to step in and take care of it, not when shifters were technically under human law like other humans.

Sam and Toby were quietly talking in the back seat, and Camden did his best not to listen to them. He doubted Toby had had much privacy when he'd been with the gang, and he wanted to give him that, and so much more. He wasn't sure where to start or what Toby would accept from him, though. It was a delicate balance, and Camden had never felt bigger and clumsier.

He had no idea where to start, both with Toby and with his mother. He suspected the easier one would be his mom, though. Whatever she thought about the way the pack should be handled, she loved him, and she respected him as an alpha.

He'd been doing this for five years, and they both knew he was good at it. He'd been learning with his father before he died, and while Camden wished he still had his guidance and that he'd learned more, he thought he was doing a decent job. Meeting Toby might throw a wrench into that, but they'd deal with it, because Camden wasn't renouncing either Toby or his alpha role.

"You're thinking too hard," Frederic murmured.

Camden checked the men behind them, but they were so focused on each other that they hadn't noticed Frederic speaking.

"I have to think. It's my job."

17

"I get that, and I get why you're so worried, but you should give yourself this evening to feel good about what happened. We saved Sam's brother, and he turned out to be your mate. I know that's not going to go down easily with some people in the pack, but their thoughts and reactions won't change what he is to you, and you'll always have me, Sam, and the others at your back. You're our alpha, but most importantly, our friend, and we want you to be happy. Honestly, I don't care who the next alpha is as long as it's a good person. He or she doesn't have to be related to you."

Camden barked out a laugh. "My mother would be appalled to hear that."

"I know, and she wouldn't be the only one. But they're the past of the pack. We're its future, and that includes you. Don't let anyone convince you that you need to sacrifice yourself and your happiness for the pack, or rather, for what they think the pack needs. You're the one deciding that, and you know better."

Camden knew he was lucky. He had his friends' support, and they'd back him through anything as long as he didn't go crazy and go against the safety and health of the pack. They wanted him to be more than an alpha, just like his father had also been a husband, a mate, a father. Camden wanted to be all that, too. He was still young, and he and Toby had just met, so they weren't going to think of children anytime soon, but he could easily imagine them being a family. Who carried their children or whether they were adopted didn't matter, because they'd be theirs, however they came into their lives.

But that was for later. Right now, Camden had to focus on Toby and on keeping him and Sam safe. He had to concentrate on his job as the alpha and on keeping the pack whole. He'd have to face his mother and deal with the fact that she'd probably refuse to talk to him for a bit, and she might try to convince him or to get someone else to convince him that his future wasn't with Toby but with a woman he needed to marry.

Camden's head was already hurting from all of that, yet he'd do it. It was his duty.

Chapter Two

Toby still wasn't used to sharing a home with his brother again. He supposed it was normal, since he'd only been with the pack a few days, but Sam wasn't the Sam he'd known before. He was quieter, and he spent a lot of time with Frederic. Toby didn't begrudge him that, but it didn't help with the feeling he had of being lost, of not belonging.

He wasn't sure he belonged anywhere anymore.

Everything was new, and with the life he'd led while with the gang, he wasn't sure how to get used to this. He was free now, but he had no idea what to do with that freedom. Having it felt overwhelming.

He'd only been eighteen when he'd been taken and when he'd lost his family. At the time, he'd had no idea what he wanted to do with his life. His parents had kept him and Sam isolated—and for excellent reasons—but they'd all known that sooner or later, they'd have left the nest to find their own way in life.

They hadn't. Sam had lived in the forest for four years, while Toby had spent that time healing gunshot and knife wounds. He'd learned to be effective and quick, and he was good at it. That didn't mean he wanted to be a healer, though. Unicorn shifters might be born healers, but that didn't mean it was what they wanted.

The problem was, Toby had no idea what he wanted.

He knew he wasn't in a rush to find out, but he still wasn't sure he could trust the pack. He wanted to, but he didn't have the same faith Sam had in them. They looked mostly like good people, that was true, and Camden was Toby's mate, but would that mean as much as Sam seemed to think when things became complicated? Toby had no way to know, and he didn't *want* things to become complicated, but that might be the only way for him to be sure he could trust the pack and Camden.

There was a knock on the bedroom door. Toby hadn't left the room much since he'd arrived, only for meals and to use the bathroom. No one had pushed him, but he knew Sam had to be becoming impatient. He had his brother back, yet he couldn't talk to him. It didn't sound fair, and it probably wasn't.

"Yes?" Toby called out.

"It's me."

Toby smiled. He might have needed some time alone, but he *wanted* to speak to his brother. "Come in."

Sam hesitantly opened and walked into the bedroom. He hovered by the door, shuffling and looking uncomfortable. It was so far from what Toby remembered of his brother, and Toby wanted that back.

He knew he wouldn't get it, though. Sam had suffered as much as him, if not more, and he wasn't the same anymore. There was no way around that.

"What are you doing? Come here," Toby said, patting the bit of mattress next to him.

Sam's smile was enough to make Toby feel better. Yes, everything was strange and uncertain, but Sam was still Sam, no matter how different he was.

Sam settled next to Toby, and they leaned against each other.

Toby took comfort in that. Maybe staying in his room wasn't the best way for him to find out what he wanted from life.

"So, you've been here a few days," Sam started.

Toby could tell he wasn't sure how to finish that sentence. "Are you trying to tell me I should start contributing?" he teased.

"No! Of course not. I know how hard this is for you. I went through it a few months ago. I was lost. I didn't know where to start. Everything was so new."

Toby patted his brother's thigh. "You're right, it *is* weird. I think I'm done with thinking, though. I'm never going to find out what I should do if I don't try to live this life."

"Maybe it would be easier for you if we went home?"

It took Toby a second to realize what Sam was talking about. It was evident to him that Sam considered the house he shared with Frederic home now, but he hadn't always. "You mean, our old home."

"Yes. We don't have to, of course, but I thought you might want to, I don't know, maybe go to Mom and Dad's grave, or see if there's anything that you can still salvage from your room. I did my best to protect the house, but part of the roof is gone, so the kitchen and the guest and master bedrooms were a loss. Your room should be okay, though, mostly. I put your clothes in plastic bags, but I left them there because I wasn't sure . . ."

"You weren't sure I'd come back."

Sam's smile was painful to look at. "Yeah. I knew Camden had found you, but I had no idea if he and the others would manage to get you out, or if you'd want to come."

"Why wouldn't I have wanted to come?"

"I don't know. We haven't seen each other in four years. I wasn't sure you didn't blame me for what happened, or —"

Toby turned to face Sam. "I don't blame you. I don't blame myself, or Mom and Dad. The only ones to blame are the people who killed them and hurt us, Sam."

Sam's answering smile was cautious. "I know. It took me a while to realize that. Sometimes, I still wonder. I'm glad you don't think I'm responsible, though." He licked his lips. "Do you want to go? I thought that maybe moving some of your old things here would help you feel more at home."

Toby *didn't* want to go, but he could see it would mean a lot to Sam, so he nodded. Besides, he could do with more clothes. He'd arrived with only the ones he'd had on his back, and while one of Sam's friends had loaned him t-shirts and jeans, Toby wanted something that was his and that he wouldn't have to give back.

Sam smiled widely. "Maybe we could shift and run there? How long has it been since you've shifted?"

"I can't remember," He hadn't been allowed when he'd been with the gang. He hadn't even been allowed to leave the house, or even his room on the days they didn't need him. They'd been too afraid he'd shift and run, and he might have, if he'd known someone was waiting for him at home in Rosewood.

They left Toby's room and went out on the porch. It was awkward to strip in front of Sam, even though Sam wasn't looking at Toby. Toby wasn't used to this anymore, to any of it. He was going to have to relearn to be a good brother, wasn't he? Sam was trying so hard, yet Toby wasn't making things easy for him.

Sam bounded down the porch steps and shifted. He shook his mane and looked at Toby, silently telling him to follow suit.

So Toby did.

Being a unicorn was freeing in a way he hadn't expected or remembered. He could stop worrying about what he was going to do or if he was being a good man and brother and *feel* — the wind in his mane as he ran, the earth and leaves under his hooves.

Forgetting about his troubles for a moment would hopefully help him deal with them once he was back in his human form. He needed to get a grip and be strong. He'd done his best for the past four years, and he couldn't break down now that he had Sam again. He needed to protect Sam and to make sure the pack wasn't using him.

Sam seemed happy there, but Toby was more cautious. He had to be. He'd seen how people could hurt him and other unicorn shifters, and he wasn't going to allow anyone to do it to Sam. Sam might have had a hard four years, but his future would be even harder if the pack manipulated and hurt him.

Toby was the youngest, but right now, he was also the strongest. He'd had to be, and he couldn't allow himself to grow soft and trusting yet, even with his mate being the pack alpha. Toby wanted to believe that Camden was as good of a man as he'd seemed and as Sam had said, but a bit of caution wouldn't hurt.

If anything, it might save him and his brother.

Camden's mother didn't know about Toby yet. Camden wasn't sure how he'd managed to keep it a secret, considering how many people had been there, although since he'd only told Frederic about Toby being his mate, maybe he shouldn't be surprised. He'd thought for sure someone would notice the particular interest he had in Toby, though. He hadn't been able to stop staring at him once they'd gotten back to the pack. They hadn't spent much time together, because Frederic had whisked both Sam and Toby back to his home while Camden dealt with the result of them sneaking into the gang's home and calling the police.

"You're nervous. Why are you nervous?"

Camden jumped, and a cloud of flour puffed up. He hadn't heard Leslie come in, and that meant he was *really* nervous and focused on his thoughts.

He glared at her. "You should knock, even though you

work in here."

"I *did* knock, but you didn't answer. I needed some files, but I think you need someone to talk to."

"I don't."

"You're baking. You usually do that when you're nervous, worried, or not looking forward to doing something. Or bored, but I don't think that applies here."

Sometimes Camden hated that Leslie knew him so well, but it couldn't be avoided. They'd grown up together — she was only one year younger than Camden's thirty-three — and she was training to be the beta once Griffin retired. Griffin had been the beta for Camden's father, and while he'd agreed to stay on for a while when Camden had taken his father's place, he was already in his fifties, and he wanted not to have to deal with the pack's skirmishes anymore. It could get tiring, but Camden didn't have the luxury of retiring, not yet. He was grateful Leslie had agreed to work with Griffin to learn the ins and outs of the job, though. Camden trusted her with his life, and possibly, with Toby's.

Of course, he'd have to talk to Toby first.

Leslie hopped onto one of the stools on the other side of the counter and leaned closer. "What kind of cookies?"

"Brownies."

"Oooh, things have to be dire, then. Not that I'm complaining, because, well, chocolate." She frowned. "But you have to know you can trust me. If I'm to be your beta once day — "

"I *do* trust you. I haven't told anyone about this, though, only Frederic." He should have told Griffin, but he was afraid of how Griffin would take it. He probably wouldn't say anything, because he realized that Camden and Leslie were the future of the pack while he was the past, but Camden disliked thinking that Griffin wouldn't look at him the same way.

"So it's a secret."

Camden shrugged and measured the sugar into the bowl

with the flour. "Not exactly. It's not going to be a secret for-ever, but I wasn't sure how to deal with it."

"Can you tell me? Do you *want* to tell me? Because if you can't—"

"Toby is my mate," Camden blurted out. Who better than Leslie to say that to right now? He was trying to gather the courage to go to his mother and tell her, but he'd finish the brownies first.

"I see," was all Leslie said.

Camden put down the chocolate and frowned at her. "That's it?"

Leslie grinned. "Pretty much. You already know I'm happy for you and that I hope you and Toby will have a perfect life. I do know why you're like this now, at least. Afraid of your mom?"

"Of course I am. I'm freaking out. You know what she thinks of this. What she'll think of Toby."

"She won't like that he has a dick rather than a vagina."

Camden grimaced, but she'd nailed the problem. "Yeah. And I don't like exerting my alpha power on her. She's my mother. She cleaned my bum when I was a kid. How am I supposed to stare her down and order her to obey me and to accept my choice when she changed my diapers?"

Leslie sighed. "I get that it isn't easy, but you're not just her son. You're the alpha, and she *has* to listen to you. Honestly, I think she will once she's bitched about Toby not being a woman. She wants the best for the pack, and she thinks a wife for you is that. But she'll realize that *Toby* is right for you, not any woman, and she'll relent. Of course, having kids for her to cuddle would probably help with that, but I doubt you're anywhere ready for that."

The thought of having to take care of children along with everything else happening in his life made Camden's heart race. "You don't think she's right? That I should forget Toby and marry a woman to ensure the future of the pack?"

"I think that's bullshit, but you already know that. You and Toby can have kids in a number of ways that don't involve you sticking your dick into a woman. Hell, I'll volunteer as a surrogate if things come to that."

Camden grimaced. "Can you *not* make me think about my dick and you, please?"

"That's what I was trying to avoid. But, Cam, seriously. Go find your mother and tell her. There's no way out of this, not if you're not planning to hide Toby forever, and I know you're not. You're not that kind of man. If you want a future with your guy, you're going to have to find your balls and use them."

She was right, which was why Camden shooed her out of his house, finished the brownies, found his balls, and went to visit his mother.

He knew she'd be home — she always was in the afternoon. She spent her mornings with Camden's sister, no doubt bemoaning the fact that neither Camden nor his brother were married and giving her grandchildren. Camden's sister had the patience of a saint, or maybe she just enjoyed using their mother as a free babysitter. Whatever the reason, Camden enjoyed not having his mother hanging around his house all day, so that was good.

The door opened before he could knock. He forced a smile on his lips and faced his mother. "Mom, hey." She had to have been peeking from behind the curtain to see he was on her porch.

"I was wondering when you'd come around."

Camden kept the smile where it was. "Yes? You know I'm busy these days."

"Yes, yes, raiding gangs and saving unicorns. I know. We don't need a second one, though. He's going to bring trouble to the pack." She stepped to the side and let Camden in.

She'd moved into this smaller house when Camden's father had died. Camden hadn't wanted her to, but she'd said that the large house belonged to the alpha and his family, not to her. It was easier to face her and tell her about Toby without the weight of the memories, though. Camden couldn't deny that.

"I'm not going to kick Toby out of the pack," he said as he followed his mother to the kitchen.

"I know you won't. Doesn't mean it's the right thing to do. Like I said, we don't need two unicorns, and he's only going to bring trouble. Mark my words."

Camden sighed. What he had to tell her wasn't going to make this better. "He's my mate, Mom."

She froze for only a second, but Camden didn't miss it. "At least now it makes sense."

"What makes sense? The fact that I'm not kicking out a twenty-two-year-old man who doesn't have anyone else on his side? He spent the past four years of life a slave to that gang. He lost his parents, and he thought he'd lost his brother, too. I'm not going to ask him to leave."

"I didn't expect you to. You're too soft-hearted, always were. How do you suppose you're going to have an heir, then? Because you're going to want to be with him, aren't you?"

"If he wants me, and there are several options we'll explore once things have settled down. I don't want to offend you, but that's none of your business, Mom."

"Of course it's not. But your father and I already had you and your sister when he was your age. You're growing old. You should start thinking about that."

"I'm only thirty-three."

"And your father was in his fifties when he died. Too young. Much too young."

Camden sighed. "I know. And I promise you, I *am* thinking

about this. I also know what's going to happen if anyone finds out about Toby and Sam. I understand the risk. But I wouldn't be a good alpha if I kicked them out. I'm sorry if it's not what you want or expected from me."

She looked at him, and to his surprise, she patted his cheek. "This might not be what I had in mind for you or what I wanted, but you're living and guiding the pack the way you think is right. Your father would be proud of you."

Why did Camden's eyes prickle with tears all of a sudden?

The only thing Toby wanted to do now that he was back at Sam and Frederic's house was to go to bed. He hadn't expected that seeing the house where he'd grown up and where his parents had died would hit him so hard. He'd thought he'd made his peace with his family's death, but being with Sam and seeing the house again had reopened the wound he'd thought had scarred over.

It hadn't.

Toby felt raw and fragile, and he was tempted to ignore the knock on the front door when he passed by it on his way upstairs from the kitchen. He could let Frederic and Sam know, but they were wrapped around each other on the couch, with Frederic murmuring things Toby didn't want to hear to Sam. Sam seemed to be as shaken as Toby felt, and Toby wanted to give him time to feel better.

So he was the one who opened the door.

He was only partly surprised to see Camden standing on the porch. He was much more surprised to see the plate in his hand. "Hi," he said, cautious.

Toby had expected Camden to come around sooner, maybe the day after he'd arrived. He'd expected Camden to push, perhaps to push him into spending time together. Instead, he was standing there looking more nervous than Toby felt, and for some reason, he was holding a plate of brownies. They smelled like heaven on earth, but that didn't tell Toby what Camden was doing there.

Camden smiled. "Hi. I made these for you."

He thrust the plate toward Toby. Toby blinked at it and took it. "For me? *You* made those?"

Camden rubbed the back of his neck and shuffled. "Yeah. I like to bake when I'm nervous."

"I make you nervous." It was obvious, but Toby had a hard time believing it. Why should Camden be nervous? Toby didn't understand it, and he didn't like not understanding people and what made them act the way they did.

"You do."

Toby had no idea what to do with Camden. He'd expected him to be harsh, maybe even hard, since he was the alpha. He needed to keep the pack safe and under control. He was no doubt used to people obeying him and doing his bidding. "Why?"

Toby's eyes widened when Camden's cheeks flushed. "Because you're you."

"Is it because I'm your mate?"

"In part, yes. I can't deny I want to make a good impression, and I don't know how to do that. I haven't dated a lot in the past five years since I became the alpha, and you're not just any guy. I want to impress you. I want you to like me, and I don't know how to do that." He shrugged, but he was still blushing. "I might be the alpha here, but that doesn't mean anything here and now."

That wasn't at all what Toby had expected from Camden, and he now realized that he'd misjudged Camden. He'd expected a lot of things from him without knowing him, and that wasn't fair.

Toby stepped to the side. "Why don't you come in? We can go to the kitchen and eat these with a glass of milk."

"Thank you." Camden followed Toby to the kitchen.

Toby didn't feel like he was home, but he needed to get used to this. He wasn't sure how long he'd be staying at Frederic and Sam's house, but it would probably be a while. He knew he was welcome there, and that Sam *wanted* him there. He needed Toby close, and that was okay, even if being there made Toby slightly uncomfortable. Besides, he'd eventually get used to living with Frederic. Sam's mate had been nothing but welcoming and easy-going, and Toby needed to relax.

He and Camden sat at the table in the kitchen after Toby had gotten the milk and glasses out. Camden pushed the plate with the brownies toward Toby, and even though he'd already had a snack, Toby took one of them. "Thank you. I'm surprised you bake. My father wouldn't have been caught dead in the kitchen, although that's mostly because he couldn't even boil water."

"It helps me relax. I have to focus on the measurements and not burning what I'm making, so I can't worry over whatever problem I'm having."

"You have a lot of them?"

"A fair share. That's the job of being an alpha. I have to keep the pack safe and be the one to help them solve the problems they might have with each other. That can go from someone accusing their neighbor of stealing the carrots from their garden to people fighting over who should inherit a house or land. It's not easy every day, and I have to be as fair as I can and ignore the fact that I grew up here and that I'm closer to some people than others."

"I see." Toby had never really thought about an alpha's job. Why should he have? He'd spent most of his life with only his family, and the following four years with a bunch of people who didn't think much of killing people.

He didn't trust people. The only person he felt comfortable

with was Sam, and he still wasn't sure Sam would be able to tell whether the pack was as good and right as it seemed to be. Sam wanted a home. He wanted a family. He wanted a place and people where he could belong, and maybe he was ready to ignore things he shouldn't ignore to get that.

Toby wasn't, though. He'd just arrived, and he didn't have any kind of feelings for the pack. He could take it or leave it. He could think about the problems that having him and Sam there might create, and he wanted to talk this out with Camden, since Camden looked like as good a man as Sam had said he was.

"You have two unicorns now," he said.

Camden swallowed his mouthful of milk and nodded. "I do. It's not a problem, though, and I don't expect you to do anything. Sam is working with our healer, and we've been trying to convince a more experience unicorn healer to come teach him what our healer can't. He wants to be a healer, and that's okay, but I don't expect that from you."

Toby nodded. "Okay. Thank you. How do I know I can trust you, though? I mean, honestly, you have to be crazy not to want to use both me and Sam. That's why the gang bought me, after all, and while I might not have had a teacher, I have four years' worth of experience on wounds you can't even imagine. Have you ever seen what a machete can do to a jaguar? Because I have, and it's not pretty."

Camden was serious now, more serious than Toby had seen him tonight. "I understand why you're not sure you can trust us. We haven't given you a reason to trust us, and you don't know us yet. You only have my word, and it's not much to you right now."

"I wish things were different."

Camden hesitated, then reached over the table and gently took Toby's hand. "I understand, Toby. I'm not offended or whatever you think. I *understand*. You've been through so much, it's incredible that you agreed to come here at all, and I know you only did it because of Sam. And that's okay. I can promise you to hell and back that I won't hurt you, but you'll only believe it with time. I truly don't expect anything from you, Toby, and by that, I mean either professionally or personally. I know we're mates, and that means a lot to me, but it *doesn't* mean you have to be with me, or that you even have to talk to me."

"It's hard to believe." Being mates meant something to Toby, too, but it didn't make it easier to trust Camden, no matter how nice and gentle he was.

"I know, and that's okay. Give it time. Just, if you can, please don't shut me out. You'll never get to know me if you refuse to talk to me. But if that's what you want, then I'll accept it. You're the one making decisions here. It's your life, and while I can offer you all the support the pack offers anyone else, I don't expect anything."

Camden wanted Toby to believe him, but he didn't think there was an easy way for him to obtain that. Toby needed time, and that was something they might not have. Camden had reached out to a few friends to find out if the news about the unicorn brothers had leaked outside their town, and so far, it didn't seem it had, but that wouldn't last long.

The only way for Camden to make sure no one found out about it would be to grab Sam and Toby and hide them somewhere, maybe in the woods where they'd lived with their parents, but he wasn't about to do that. They both deserved a life, a real one, and he wanted to give that to them.

Of course, they wouldn't have it if they were kidnapped, but Camden didn't think that would happen, not at first anyway. If someone found out about them, they'd contact Camden and offer to pay him, probably along with threatening him a bit. He had experience as alpha, but he was still only thirty-three, and some people would think that meant he was easily influenceable. They'd get a nasty surprise when they realized he wasn't.

"I'll give you and your pack a chance," Toby finally said.

"That's all I'm asking." Camden was relieved Toby was ready to give him that. He'd half expected his mate to say fuck it, grab Sam, and leave. They hadn't had the best experience with shifters, and while Sam had spent enough time with the pack to know he and Toby were safe here, Toby was understandably more guarded.

"You haven't forced my brother to become a healer?" Toby sounded like he didn't quite believe that.

Camden was perplexed because he'd thought Sam had talked to his brother, but maybe he hadn't, or maybe Toby was trying to make sure he hadn't lied.

"I wouldn't force him or anyone else to do anything they didn't want."

"He's a unicorn. That's what we do. We heal."

"You can, yes. You can also decide you don't want to bother with humans and become a veterinarian. You can decide you don't want anything to do with healing and become, I don't know, a car mechanic, or open a store. You can become a writer or a painter. I don't care. That's something *you* are going to have to decide. I want you to know that you can do that here. You can take the time to think about your options."

Toby's eyes were narrowed, but he seemed less wary than he'd been in the beginning. Maybe it was Camden's charm, or maybe it was the brownies. Whatever the reason, Camden was happy about it.

He wanted to stay and spend more time with Toby, but he suspected that wouldn't be welcome, not yet, so he got up. Toby blinked at him but followed his lead.

"What are you doing?" Toby asked.

"I'm leaving."

"Why?"

Camden smiled. "I know you didn't ask me to, but I think you probably want some time to think everything over and decide whether you can risk trusting me or not."

Toby's cheeks flushed, but he was unapologetic when he said, "You're right. I do want to think about what was said this evening."

"You know where to find me if you need anything?"

"Sam told me which one your house is."

"Good. And when I say anything, I do mean *anything*. Just come around, okay? Even if I'm not home, you're welcome to go in and wait for me."

"I couldn't do that. It's your home."

Camden stopped next to the front door. "It is." He decided to take a risk. "And one day, I hope it will be yours, too. I'd like you to be comfortable there." He leaned forward and, without touching Toby with his hands or any other parts of his body, he kissed Toby's cheek. It was maybe a bit too close to the corner of his lips, but Camden hadn't been able to resist, and Toby didn't seem to mind. He didn't push Camden away — rather, he moved closer. He didn't touch Camden, but he didn't need to. Camden was already backing off and watching him to make sure he hadn't overstepped.

Camden smiled. "Goodnight, Toby."

Toby touched his cheek and blinked. "Goodnight."

Camden had to force himself to leave. He wanted nothing more than to stay and beg Toby to trust him, but things didn't work like that. Nothing he could do or say would make Toby trust him. It was something Toby had to feel, and he was the only one who could do that.

Camden also didn't look back. He didn't want to find out whether Toby was watching him walk away. He'd be sad if Toby wasn't, but if he was, Camden would be tempted to go back, and that wasn't something he could afford right now. He didn't want to do anything that might put his budding relationship with Toby in danger, or worse, that might put Toby's *life* in danger. There was no way to know how Toby might react if Camden pushed too hard, too fast, and Camden didn't want to find out by experimenting.

He walked home, feeling exhausted. Between the raid on the gang, finding Toby, talking to his mother, and worrying about everything, he was ready for a good night's sleep.

So of course, he found his brother waiting on the swing he kept on the porch.

Camden groaned. "What are you doing here?" he asked Bryson, making a beeline for the front door and hoping Bryson would leave when he noticed Camden didn't want him there.

Bryson rose. Even though he was younger than Camden by five years, he was bigger than Camden, and not only in height. He looked more like an alpha than Camden, but he'd never wanted the charge, and Camden didn't blame him.

"Mom called me," Bryson said.

Camden should have expected that, but he hadn't thought much about it after he'd left his mother's house. "Of course she did. Come on. I need a beer."

"When were you going to tell Vic and me? *Were* you going to tell us about your *mate*?"

"For fuck sake, Bry. Of course I was going to tell you. I didn't tell anyone but Frederic until today, and he only knew because he was there when I met Toby and because Toby is Sam's brother. Give me a break, yeah? Things are more complicated than I'd like and than I'm comfortable with."

"Because he's a unicorn," Bryson said, flopping into one of the stools at the kitchen counter and making grabby hands when Camden took a beer out of the fridge.

Camden rolled his eyes and handed it to his brother, then

took a second bottle. "Because of that yeah, mostly."

"And because he doesn't have the right plumbing to give Mom the grandkids she wants from you."

"She didn't seem to mind too much when I told her earlier."

Bryson grimaced. "That's because she knows there's nothing she can do or say to make you change your mind. You're too honorable, or something like that. But she talked my ears off when she called me. She told me all about how wrong Toby is for you and how he's going to bring the pack trouble." He grinned. "I took that as meaning that he's perfect for you."

Camden sighed in relief. "I don't know that he is, but I hope so."

"Of course he is. He's your mate, isn't he? There's no one else as perfect for you in the world and all that crap."

"All that crap, huh? Wait until *you* meet your mate."

"I don't know that I will. That stuff is rare."

"It's certainly supposed to be, but Frederic met his, then me. Looks like it might become an epidemic or something."

Bryson visibly shuddered. "God, I hope not. I'm nowhere ready to get married."

"Nothing says you have to get married if you meet your mate, now or ever."

"Because you're not dying to put a ring on your man's finger?"

The thought was as exhilarating as it was terrifying. "Maybe, but it's going to take a while. Toby doesn't trust anyone but his brother right now, and I doubt that's going to change anytime soon."

"Maybe it's not, but you've always been stubborn. You'll wear him down eventually, and you'll live in utter bliss, making all of us wish we could bleach our eyeballs for having to watch the two of you make eyes at each other."

That sounded like the perfect future, but Camden was

almost afraid to let himself hope. Even if he did manage to get Toby to trust him, dangers were lurking outside the pack, and they might still bowl them over and take over their lives.

CHAPTER THREE

Toby still wasn't sure he wanted to become a healer — or continue to be one, as it was — but going with Sam to meet the pack healer was better than staying home alone. He'd had enough of that over the past week. It was time to get his ass out and start living now that he had the chance to do so.

"She's a good person, you'll see," Sam said.

"I believe you."

"She can be a bit intimidating, though. She speaks her mind. She's not afraid to tell you what she thinks about you right off the bat."

"She sounds like a lovely lady," Toby teased. He had no idea what to think of Naila, but Sam seemed to like her, and they were about to see her, so Toby would be able to form his own opinion. The way he saw it, anyone who'd welcomed his brother and was helping him was probably a good person, but he was still cautious with the pack.

Most of the people were nice. A few obviously avoided Sam and Toby, but Toby didn't care. He didn't want to be friends with people who didn't want him there. He had enough people in his life with Sam, his mate, and their friends. Some days, they felt like too much, but Toby was aware of the fact that this was his problem, not theirs.

"You're still not sure if you want to be a healer?" Sam asked.

Toby wasn't sure what to tell him. "I was forced to be one for the past four years."

"I know, and I know it's probably not what you had in

mind when you thought about the future. But we're unicorn shifters, and while I don't want you to do something you hate, I also think that the four years of experience you have could be useful." He hesitated. "Especially if the pack ends up with trouble because of us."

Toby grimaced. It *was* true that his experience would probably be useful, even though he didn't have any formal training. He'd been thrown into the job when the gang had bought him, and he'd had to learn that way. This was his chance to refine the skills he already had. Even if he decided he couldn't stay with the pack, it would be useful for him. He could find a job if he knew what he was doing, even if it wasn't the job of his dreams. And he couldn't deny that maybe he ought to repay the pack in some way. They were paying for his food and everything else because he didn't have anything—or rather, Frederic was. Toby wasn't sure how to thank him. He wasn't sure he could, not until he found himself a job.

"I didn't ask the pack to find me," Toby pointed out. He didn't want to antagonize Sam, but he still wasn't sure the pack was trustworthy. It was easy for them to welcome him and Sam now, while no one knew about them, but what about when people realized they could get their hands on a unicorn shifter? The pack was going to have to choose between handing Sam or Toby over, or protecting them and face the consequences of that, and Toby wasn't sure which option they'd choose.

Maybe Camden would try to keep him, since they were mates, but Sam would leave this place over Toby's dead body. Toby didn't care about being the alpha's husband or about helping Camden deal with the pack. He didn't want to do that, even though he knew it was exactly what he'd end up with if he decided he wanted Camden in his life.

But all this thinking over this would be a moot point unless Toby was sure both he and Sam would be safe with the pack, and he couldn't be yet. He was still waiting for the other shoe to drop, and it was going to. He was sure of that. Which way it would drop was an unknown, though.

Sam sighed as they got to a small cottage set further in the forest than the rest of the houses that made up the tiny village where the pack lived. "You can trust Camden, you know," he said.

"I want to."

"But you don't think you can."

"Not yet. As you said, someone is bound to find out about us, and when that happens, the pack will be in trouble. There's no way for us to know how the pack will react to that, and I'm not ready to believe they won't hand one of us over. I'm not sure which one—I'm the alpha's mate, but you've been here for longer."

"They won't hand off either of us. I'm sure of that."

"I know." Toby wished he could be just as sure.

"But you're not. You'll see, in time. I was as distrustful as you in the beginning. I spent the past four years in the forest on my own, and I had no idea who I could trust when I met Frederic and the pack. But I had to take that first step, and they've only been good to me."

But they hadn't had to *choose*. Sam wouldn't understand that. He'd spent years in the forest, and before that, the two of them and their parents had lived isolated. Sam had no idea how dangerous and *bad* people could be, even though he'd had to live through the death of their parents. He wanted to see the good in people, but Toby had seen the worst in them.

He couldn't deny it existed.

The cottage door opened, and an older woman stood there, watching them. For some reason, Toby had imagined her to appear elderly, with white hair and looking grandma-like. She was older, but not as much as he'd thought. Her hair was braided and was starting to go white, but she was tall, taller than Toby, and she stood straight and strong-looking.

"It's about time you two got here," she said when they were closer.

Sam smiled at her. He trusted her—Toby could see it in the way he looked at her. "Sorry. Toby wasn't sure what he wanted to do."

Toby scowled at him. "Are you trying to put the blame on me?"

"Why not? It *was* your fault."

"I don't care whose fault it was," Naila said. Her voice had a harsh edge, but it was also amused. "Sam, you need to gather the herbs for drying. Summer won't stay here for much longer, and I want to be sure I have enough of them for the winter."

Toby couldn't miss how much surer of himself Sam looked and moved now. He knew precisely what Naila wanted from him, and he jumped into action, giving Toby one last smile before heading toward the cottage.

Toby had no idea what to do now that he was left alone with Naila. He didn't even know if he wanted her help.

She moved until she stood in front of him. "I can't say I ever thought I'd have to teach two unicorn shifters to heal."

"I know how to heal. I spent the past four years doing it." So he was defensive. Who wouldn't be in his situation?

"Sure you do. Your brother did, too, when he arrived. Do you know what we use rosemary for?"

Toby frowned. "I never used rosemary when I healed."

"What did you heal, then?"

"Mostly gunshots and knife wounds."

"I see. No fevers? Other illnesses?"

"No. The gang who bought me didn't use me for their colds."

"So you couldn't heal that? Or a fever? The flu?"

"No." Toby had never thought about how limited his

power was. He hadn't *needed* to know how to deal with that stuff before.

"Do you want to learn?"

"I'm not sure."

"Mmm. What are you doing here, then?"

"I'm not sure of that, either."

"You don't seem sure of much right now. Will you stay with the pack?"

"Do you need me to? Do you *want* me to?"

"That's not what I asked, is it? I can't deny I'm looking at taking a step back from the position as a pack healer, but I won't do that until I'm sure Sam is ready to take things on his own. Having someone to help would be useful."

"Does the pack need two healers?"

"Possibly. The pack is expanding, even though it's still small. We have a lot of small children and newborns and pregnant women. That means the work is going to grow in the next few years. Sam *could* do it on his own, but I don't see why he should. Being a healer isn't always easy, and I didn't have the support I needed more than once. There's the possibility Sam could have it, so why not? Although of course, you have to want it, too."

And that was the crux of it, wasn't it? What did Toby want?

Camden knew something was wrong when Griffin barged into his office without knocking. Griffin would have never done that if whatever had happened wasn't urgent, and Camden's stomach churned with anxiousness.

"What's wrong?" he asked, rising from his chair behind the desk.

Griffin stopped in front of Camden. "An envoy from the Springfield pack is demanding to talk to you."

Camden swallowed and sat back in his chair. The

Springfield pack was bigger than his pack. It was close to a bigger town, and as such, they had more resources. Camden was perfectly happy with his pack and how many members it had, but the fact that they were so small did put him at a disadvantage right now. "He's here because of Sam and Toby."

It wasn't a question, but Griffin answered anyway. "That's my guess. He hasn't told me, but I don't see why else he should be here. There's no reason for him to be."

Camden rubbed his face. He'd known this was coming, but he still had no idea how to deal with it. "Bring him here. And can you ask Leslie to come, too? I want her to be here."

"Are you sure that's a good idea? She still has trouble not blurting out what she thinks sometimes, and I don't want that to happen, not in this situation."

"I need all the support I can get, and this is a prime moment for her to learn, isn't it?"

Griffin nodded, but Camden could see he had something on his mind. He wasn't surprised when Griffin asked, "You still aren't going to give up one of the brothers, are you?"

"I'm not. They're not animals to sell or trade. They're humans, both of them, and they belong wherever they want to belong."

Griffin nodded. "I'll let the envoy in and call Leslie."

"Give the man some water and wait until she's here to lead him to my office." That way, Camden would have a moment to gather his thoughts.

He had no idea how to deal with this, but he couldn't let that show. Any hint of weakness would be revealing, too much so. Sam and Toby were with the Rosewood pack to stay, and that was that. Now Camden had to find a way to make sure it happened.

The Springfield pack had the means to pressure him, though. They could attack the pack and take what they wanted. The reason they hadn't so far was that they probably didn't want the reputation of being a ruthless pack that didn't even try the diplomacy way before barging in. Besides, they probably also didn't want the other packs in the area to find out *why* they were doing this. Camden didn't know how they'd found out about Sam and Toby, but they probably couldn't risk another pack taking notice and trying to get to the coveted unicorn shifters before them.

This was a fucking mess.

Camden was relieved when Leslie rushed in. "What are we going to do?" she asked as she came to stand next to him. Griffin would do the same on Camden's other side when he arrived, and together, they'd present a united front.

"I have no idea." Camden wasn't sure he should be admitting that, but he trusted Griffin and Leslie, enough to show them how vulnerable he was right now. He couldn't give up Toby, and he couldn't ask Toby and Frederic to give up Sam. Even if the brothers hadn't been mates to pack members, though, Camden wouldn't have allowed them to be taken. They weren't animals. They were human beings, and they were the only ones who should decide what they wanted with their lives.

"We're not going to let anyone take Toby and Sam, right?"

"Of course not." There was one thing Camden was sure of, and it was this one.

Griffin knocked on the door a few minutes later, and Camden called for him to come in. He did, followed by a man Camden had never met.

His pack and the ones in the towns and cities in the area didn't mingle. He knew the alphas, of course, since they kept each other informed of what was going on, but they weren't friends, for the most part. Camden *did* have a few alphas he was closer to, but they weren't involved in this case, and he wasn't sure they would agree to help even if he asked. No one wanted to get the attention of stronger packs. They couldn't afford it, especially not when their pack members were mostly people who'd never fought and who wouldn't know where to start.

"Alpha Cook," the man said, stopping in front of Camden.

Camden gestured at the chair on the other side of his desk. "Please, sit."

The man nodded. He settled into the chair, and Camden waited until Griffin had come to stand behind him to ask, "To what do I owe this visit?

"My name is John Harris. My alpha, Alpha Wilson, sent me to discuss the selling of one of your unicorn shifters."

The bottom of Camden's stomach dropped, but he made sure his expression gave none of the dread he felt away. "Sam and Toby aren't for sale."

"Are you saying my pack is welcome to take one of them?"

"No. I'm saying that they're adult men who can decide whether they want to live with my pack or move in with yours. They're human beings, not animals you or anyone else can buy."

The smile Harris gave Camden made Camden's skin crawl. "Of course you'd say that. You have two of them. But you know as well as I do what will happen if you insist on not sharing your wealth."

Camden gritted his teeth. "I'm sure you know my pack isn't wealthy."

"I know. That's why Alpha Wilson thought you'd welcome an offer. We don't care which unicorn you give us. You can choose. But we're not going to take no for an answer."

Camden had already known that, and he suspected that whatever he said, it would never be enough for this man and his alpha to see what he was trying to say. They thought of Sam and Toby as things to use for their gain, not as human beings who shouldn't be trafficked. Nothing Camden could say would change their minds.

Camden had to find a way out of this, though. "As I said, you're welcome to ask them if they want to move in with your pack, although I doubt they will. Toby is my mate, while Sam is the mate of one of my pack members and best friend. Considering the way you talk about them, I don't see why they should want to live with your pack in this situation."

"They'll probably change their mind when they realize that my pack has more members and that we can take yours out easily. We don't want to use violence, but we will if you don't accept our offer. Of course, we are ready to give you some time to think about it. You'll want to talk things out with your beta and the unicorns. But we're not going to back off, and we're not going to give you months to decide. You should start thinking about what you're ready to sacrifice for your pack."

"I won't sacrifice my mate," Camden snapped. It didn't matter that Toby might decide he didn't want him. Both Toby and Sam deserved to be free.

"Then give us the other one."

"Sam has a mate, and Frederic won't allow you to hurt Sam."

"Of course not. We don't want the unicorn to hurt him. We need him for his healing power."

"And you're ready to treat him like an animal to get that. I thought shifters were well aware of the way that feels, since humans see us as little more than our animals."

Harris waved Camden's words away. "I don't care about humans, and what they think doesn't make a difference. Look, it's simple. You have two unicorns. We want one of them. We don't care which one. We're ready to pay you for him, and we're giving you a few days to think things over and tell us your price. If you still refuse once my alpha's patience runs out, we'll take him by force. I'm sure you don't want to be remembered as the alpha who valued a single unicorn over his entire pack."

Camden didn't want that, of course, but he also didn't want to be remembered as the alpha who was ready to sell another human being to keep his pack safe. What kind of a monster would that make him?

"What did you think?" Sam asked as he and Toby trudged home.

Trudged might be a bit of an exaggeration, but Toby was so tired that it certainly felt like that was what he was doing. Naila hadn't given him time to rest once he'd decided to stay and see what would happen. He still had no idea what he wanted to do, even though he was already decent at healing, but he wanted to spend time with Sam, and working alongside with him helped with that.

They'd chatted as they gathered herbs to dry, and it had been like when they were kids. Toby remembered their mom doing that very same thing, since they only went into town when they had no other choice. She'd probably healed Toby and Sam's childhood illnesses with the herbs from her garden, and Toby wished he remembered more of that. Maybe working with Naila could be like using his mom's legacy in a way.

There was no downside to it that he could see, except the one that he wasn't sure it was what he wanted to do for the rest of his life—which was kind of ridiculous, because who did? Toby could learn to heal and change his mind in five or ten years, then do something else.

He had endless possibilities now that he was free, and while feeling like he didn't know what he was doing was terrifying, it was also a relief. He could stay with Sam. He *wanted* to stay with Sam. Whether or not they'd stay with the pack,

Toby wasn't sure, although he suspected he'd have trouble getting Sam away from Frederic. Those two were starting their relationship, but Sam was already in love with his mate. Toby could see it.

He didn't want to hurt Sam or to freak him out, so he was cautious when he answered, "She's certainly special."

Sam laughed. "Don't let her hear that you think that. She'd kick your ass."

"Don't you find it overwhelming? The pack, a new house, a mate, a job. I don't know where to start, but you seem to have everything under control."

"Oh, I don't. Sometimes I stay up at night worrying, wondering if I'm doing the right thing by staying here. I know our presence endangers the pack, and Frederic has suggested we could leave, but his family is here. This is where he grew up, and I know he doesn't want to leave, even though he'd do it to keep me safe. But I like it here."

"Even though it's so close to the place where we grew up?"

"Maybe because of that. I'm still sad when I think of Mom and Dad, and I avoid doing it too much, especially their deaths, but this is our home, you know? Even though we grew up in the forest rather than with the pack, it's still home, and we have a place here. I don't want to leave. I want to be happy here, and I think I have a chance at that." He hesitated. "But you should go if you don't think *you* do."

"I want to be with you."

"I know. That doesn't mean it's the right thing for you, though. I know that being Camden's mate complicates things, and I don't want to push you in any way when it comes to him, but he's a good man."

Toby couldn't help but smile. "And you think I should give him a chance."

"Well, I'd like to see both of you happy, and I do think you can be together. It's obvious you're not comfortable here, though."

"Were you comfortable right away when you arrived?"

"No. But I also didn't close myself off."

"I'm not doing that."

"Not with everyone. Not with me. But I know you and Camden aren't talking, and you'll never get to know him if you don't give him a chance. Being in a relationship isn't the only way to be happy, far from it, but I like feeling like someone loves me for who I am. Frederic does. He never pushes, never demands anything I'm not ready to give him, but having him in my life, well, it *does* make things easier. I know I have someone I can lean on, someone who will support me and help me if I need it. I think that's what I missed the most when I was on my own." He chuckled. "Well, that, and donuts."

"You've always had a sweet tooth." Toby understood what Sam was saying, though. He was *lonely*. Even with Sam and Frederic in his life, Toby felt like he didn't have something for himself, *someone* for him, the way Sam had Frederic. And the stupid part was that he could have it if he gave Camden a chance.

He just had to make that decision.

"Sam!"

Sam and Toby both looked up. Sage, Sam's friend, was rushing toward them. Toby frowned when he noticed Sage looked frazzled. He was usually so sweet and nice and gentle.

"Did something happen?" Sam asked when they'd gotten close enough for Sage to answer without yelling.

"Yes. You two have to be careful. There was an envoy, from another pack."

Toby's stomach churned. He knew what had happened. He'd known it would happen sooner or later. "What did he want?" he asked anyway.

"He asked Camden for one of you."

And while Camden had probably said no, and might continue to say no, he'd eventually give in. He was the alpha. He needed to keep his pack safe, and that wouldn't happen if he kept two unicorns. Hell, some packs wouldn't have a problem taking both Sam and Toby, and Camden wouldn't be able to do anything about it.

Toby and Sam needed to leave.

Toby grabbed Sam's hand and dragged him toward the house.

"What are you doing?" Sam asked as he tried to free himself.

How could he not understand what was at stake? What they had to do? "We need to pack. Not much, but enough that we have a few days' worth of food."

"What are you talking about, Toby?"

Toby stopped and turned to face Sam. "We have to go."

Sam shook his head. "Why?"

"Because Camden is going to give up one of us sooner or later, whether he wants it or not." And Toby still wasn't convinced he didn't want it. For all that Camden was his mate, they didn't know each other, and while that was Toby's fault, right now, it didn't change the facts.

Sam stepped back. "He won't."

"He's going to have to, Sam. Can't you see? They're going to give him a choice if they haven't already — one of us against the safety of the pack. They wouldn't have come if they weren't sure they could get what they want. Camden is going to give in because he wants his pack to be safe." As was right. He wouldn't be the alpha if he didn't think about the pack's wellbeing.

"You're wrong. He'll find a way. He promised you he wouldn't allow anyone to hurt either of us, and he's going to keep that promise. You'd know that if you'd let him in."

Toby shook his head. He turned and walked toward the

house, already mentally thinking about what would fit in his backpack. He couldn't force Sam to come with him, even though he didn't like the thought of leaving him behind. But maybe Sam would be safe once Toby was gone. If the pack only had one unicorn, they wouldn't have to give him up. Toby couldn't be sure of that, but panic gripped him.

He wasn't going to let anyone sell him like a piece of meat ever again. He'd already gone through that once, and he wouldn't survive a second time.

"Toby! What are you doing?" Sam called out behind him.

Toby didn't stop to explain. It was going to become evident once he left the house and ran into the woods anyway.

He'd shift into his unicorn form. He'd be faster that way, and he'd be able to get farther away than he could in his human form. Maybe he could stop somewhere for the night if he had enough money, but otherwise, he'd sleep in his unicorn form in the woods.

He had a plan. He hated leaving his brother behind, but Sam had been alone for four years. He could defend himself. Besides, he wasn't alone anymore, and if there was one thing he was sure of, it was that Frederic loved Sam and that he wouldn't allow anyone to take him away or to hurt him.

Someone was pounding on Camden's door, and he wasn't sure he wanted to answer.

He had enough to deal with right now as it was. He'd started calling all the alphas and friends he could think of after the Springfield envoy had left, and while they were all sorry for what he was going through, they couldn't help. They couldn't afford to. The Springfield pack wasn't huge, but other packs backed it, and no one wanted to antagonize those.

So Camden was alone in this.

He'd sent Leslie and Griffin home. Their presence

wouldn't help. Neither of them had managed to come up with a solution, and honestly, Camden wasn't sure there was one. The Springfield pack wasn't going to back down. They wanted Sam or Toby, by any means necessary.

Maybe answering the door would be a welcome distraction.

Camden knew he was wrong to think that as soon as he opened and saw Sage's frantic expression. "What happened now?" he asked with a growl. He wasn't angry with Sage, but he wasn't sure he could deal with anything else.

"It's Toby."

Camden's heart stopped. "Toby?"

"I told him and Sam about the envoy. I thought they should know, but I didn't expect Toby to react the way he did."

"What did he do?"

"He went straight to his bedroom to start packing. He thinks you're going to give either him or Sam up because you'll have to to keep the pack safe. He won't listen, no matter how many times Sam and I tell him he's wrong."

"Shit."

"I thought you might be able to change his mind, since you're the alpha and his mate."

Camden grabbed his jacket and shrugged it on as he left the house. "The news has already gone around?"

"Frederic told Reece, who told me. Oh, and Bryson texted me, too."

"I hate all of them."

"No, you don't." Sage bit his lower lip. "What are you going to do?"

"I'm going to tell Toby I'm not about to sell him or his brother."

"I know that. I meant about the Springfield pack."

Camden sighed. "I have no idea. I've been making calls for help, but so far, I haven't had any luck with that." He didn't need to tell Sage what would happen if he didn't find anyone and if he didn't hand off Toby or Sam. The fact that he'd asked meant he already knew, and Camden suspected most of the pack did.

What *was* he going to do if no one stepped in to help? He couldn't give up Toby or Sam, but he also couldn't allow the pack to get hurt. He doubted the pack members would let that happen anyway. Knowing some of them, they'd grab the brothers and hand them off themselves even though they knew Camden wouldn't be okay with that. They'd go around him, and no amount of yelling or consequences would change what they would have done.

No, Camden couldn't allow that. He wasn't quite sure what the alternative was, but he'd find one. He had to.

He and Sage got to Frederic's house, where they found Sam pacing the porch. When he noticed them, he pointed at the forest. "He shifted and left. I wanted to follow him, but then you wouldn't have been able to find us, and I know that nothing I can say will reassure him."

Camden nodded. He was already stripping, and once he was in his wolf form, he didn't have trouble finding Toby's trace.

Toby smelled of horse and the woods, and of Camden's mate. It made Camden's heart ache, but he pushed that away and followed the lead into the woods. Sage and Sam stayed behind, thank God. Camden wasn't sure he'd have managed to keep an eye on them while running to find Toby. Toby was a unicorn shifter, a horse, so he'd be fast in that form. Camden was slower, but not so slow that he couldn't catch up. He knew his territory, and his nose was better than Toby's. Toby would need a moment to gather his wits and to decide which way to go. Camden didn't. He only had to follow Toby's scent.

He found his mate at the stream where Frederic had first

met Sam. He was drinking, his backpack hanging from his neck. He was magnificent in this form, tall and strong, his white coat shining in the moonlight. His horn made him lethal, and Camden hoped he wasn't so angry that he wouldn't listen.

He shifted. It was fucking cold, and he hoped Toby wouldn't notice the shrinkage. Not that it would matter if he did. The only thing Camden wanted was for Toby to come home and to keep him safe, and if things came to that, he'd take his mate, and they'd leave together.

That knowledge knocked the air out of Camden's lungs. He was ready to do anything to save his mate, including leaving the pack. Griffin would be a good alpha if he needed to step up, and Leslie could help him. Toby was more important to Camden than the pack, and he knew that the Springfield pack would only leave them alone if Toby was gone.

"Toby?" he called out.

Toby snapped his head toward Camden. Camden held his hands up to show him he wasn't armed. "I don't have anything with me, as you can see." There were no places where he could have hidden anything. "I need you to listen to me, please."

Camden held his breath as he waited for Toby to make his decision.

Toby stepped closer. He didn't shift, but Camden had the impression that he was waiting for him to speak, so he did.

"I know you're afraid. I am, too. I'm terrified of what will happen to the pack if I don't give in. I wasn't ready to become the alpha when my father died, and I'm not sure I am now. I don't want the pack to be hurt by my decisions, but that doesn't change the fact that I am *not* going to sell you or hand you over to the Springfield pack. You are not animals to be sold. You are the one who decides what you want to do, and if you want to leave once I'm done talking, then I won't stop you."

Toby neighed softly. Camden took it as a signal to continue.

"I called several friends, and I have more to contact. I'm hoping someone will send help to keep the Springfield pack at bay. If they don't and I have to choose between the pack and you, I'll choose you. We can leave so the Springfield pack won't have a reason to attack. Maybe we can convince Sam and Frederic to come with us. And yes, I would leave the pack, my family, and my alpha position for you. I wouldn't even have to think about it, and I wouldn't regret it. I promise you that. Give me some time to try, though. Please. I don't want you to have to leave your brother behind, not now that you finally have him again. And I don't want to lose you. I know you haven't made a decision when it comes to me, and that's okay. Even if we leave together, you won't owe me anything, I promise. I'd like a chance, though."

Camden wasn't sure what to expect when Toby shifted. He did his best not to stare at Toby's naked body, moving his focus to Toby's face.

"What about the other packs? The ones that will come after the Springfield pack? Even if you do manage to push back against Springfield, now that the word is out, others will come for Sam and me. What will you do then?"

"I don't know. We'll see once we get there, I guess. But now that we know, and once the Springfield pack is dealt with, we can make more plans accordingly."

Camden had no idea how they'd do that, but they needed to focus on the problem at hand before thinking about issues that might not arise. Toby was no doubt right when he said that others would come, but for now, they hadn't, while the Springfield pack had. That was who they needed to focus on. That was the biggest danger now.

"I don't know how to stop running," Toby murmured.

"I'm scared. I'm *terrified*. I never had anyone I could trust apart from my parents and my brother."

"Then trust Sam. He's scared, too, but he trusts me, and I promise you that if I think we won't be able to do this, we'll leave. I won't allow the Springfield pack to get their hands on you or Sam."

He wouldn't allow it, be it the last thing he did.

CHAPTER FOUR

Toby still hadn't unpacked his backpack. He couldn't seem to bring himself to do it, even with Camden's reassurance that he was doing everything he could to keep the Springfield pack away.

It had only been a few days, and Toby knew that eventually, the Springfield pack would win. Whether that meant that he'd leave alone or with Sam, or with Camden, he didn't know, but something had to happen, and not knowing what or when was terrifying.

He'd had time to think things over. Camden was spending his days on the phone trying to find help, so he hadn't had time for Toby. Toby was kind of sorry. He barely knew his mate, and the situation wasn't the greatest, but in a perfect world, he thought he'd fall in love with Camden.

Toby didn't know if he trusted Camden, but he could see how hard his mate was trying. He needed to keep the pack safe, and he wanted to give Toby a free life. Those two goals conflicted with each other, though, and he was having a hard time finding balance. They all were.

Toby was torn between wanting to stay with Sam and Camden and leaving to make sure they'd both be safe. He knew that would be the smartest thing to do, but he'd thought his brother was dead for four years. Was it selfish to want to spend time with him now? To stay with the pack? Toby had thought he wouldn't want that, but now that he faced having to leave, he realized he'd started settling down, and he wanted to stay.

He sighed and pressed his forehead against his bedroom window. He knew it was ridiculous to stay there and watch for the Springfield pack envoy. The man wasn't going to storm the pack yet. They had another few days, maybe more, and Camden hadn't lost hope that he'd find someone who could help. Toby wasn't sure he shared that hope, but he couldn't help but wish.

He wasn't a pack member yet, not the way Sam was. Sam had made friends. He was studying with the healer. He was making this place his home and building a family, and while Toby knew he had a place there, he couldn't help but feel like he'd take something away from his brother if he stayed. Sam didn't want him to go, but was there really an alternative?

"You're still watching for the envoy," Sam said from the open bedroom door.

Toby didn't turn to look at him. "Yes. I need to be sure you're safe."

"You know, I'm older than you. I should be the one protecting you, not the other way around."

Toby snorted. "Being older doesn't have anything to do with it. I had to become strong when I was with the gang while you were all alone in the forest. You're softer, and that's not a bad thing. I don't want you to be hardened by life the way I was."

Sam sat on the bench under the window next to Toby. "I hate this, though."

"I do too. There's not much we can do about the past, though."

"But we can change the future. I know you're afraid. I am, too. But we can't lose hope. I want you to be in my life. I was alone for so long, and now I feel complete."

"You don't need me. You have Frederic and Sage, and Reece, and —"

Sam grabbed Toby's hand and squeezed. "I know I have

them. They're important to me. They make me feel like I belong here, and that's good. It doesn't mean that I wouldn't feel your absence, though. I don't want you to leave. I want you to stay and marry Camden, have kids, and be happy. I know it sounds like a utopia, but I spent four years dreaming about this when I was alone in the forest. About finding you again, and about having a family. I'm not going to let anyone destroy my dream by taking away a piece of it."

"It would be safer for both of us."

Sam sighed and leaned his forehead against Toby's shoulder. "I hate this situation."

"I do, too." Toby hadn't thought everything was going to be perfect once he was rescued from the gang. Most days, he hadn't even allowed himself to dream such a thing might happen. He hadn't wanted to hope.

But there he was, and he was in danger of losing everything again. He didn't want it to happen, but what was he supposed to do? Staying was out of the question if Camden didn't find a way to protect the pack. Leaving would hurt like hell, but at least both Toby, Sam, and everyone else would be safe. No matter how little Toby wanted that to happen, it looked like it was the way things would go.

"You could marry Camden," Sam said.

Toby blinked. "What?"

Sam straightened and turned to face Toby. "Think about it. The fact that you're Camden's mate already means a lot, right? I mean, he's an alpha, and shifters tend to respect being mates anyway. I'm not surprised they're considering taking you away, considering what we are, but maybe if you and Camden were married, they wouldn't. It's not like they could separate a married couple, not when one of the men is an alpha."

Toby's stomach churned. "What about you, though? Even if Camden did agree with this, and I don't know that he would, it would leave you vulnerable. Right now, Camden is ready to run away with me to make sure we're both safe. He thinks that once I'm gone, the Springfield pack will leave you alone. They won't have the excuse that this pack has two unicorn shifters, and since you're training to become the next healer, Camden doesn't think they'd try to take you away. But if I marry him and I'm out of reach to them, things might change, especially since you and Frederic *aren't* married."

Sam bit his lower lip. "We could be."

"You want to wait. You're not ready."

"Maybe not, not entirely, but I'm also not ready to be kidnapped by another pack. Where would that leave me? I know Camden and Frederic would come after me, and they'd probably get hurt in the process. I also know that while I still feel unsure of this life, Frederic isn't going anywhere. The fact that he's my mate doesn't matter as much as the fact that he's a good man and that I'm in love with him. I don't know if I'll *ever* feel ready to get married, even though I know he loves me too. It feels like a huge step to take after spending all my life with only three people. But I'm ready to take it if it means keeping myself and you safe."

Toby didn't know what to say. He'd thought about this, of course, but he'd dismissed it as impractical and dangerous for Sam. Would Sam and Frederic's wedding change things, though? Sam wasn't wrong when he said that no pack would try to separate married couples, especially not if they were also soul mates. They might try to get both Frederic and Sam, but they'd have to fight them. Neither would go willingly, and Sam was stronger than he appeared at first sight.

Toby had no way to be sure that marrying Camden would solve the problem or make it easier or harder to deal with. He had no way to be sure that Sam marrying Frederic would change anything. What else could they do, though? They could wait and hope someone would help. They could plan for when they possibly had to leave. But those two weddings might help, and Toby couldn't ignore that.

Was he ready to marry Camden? No. He was nowhere near ready to take that big of a step. He barely knew the man, and that was mostly his own fault. He shouldn't have isolated himself and pushed everyone but Sam away when he'd gotten here. He'd been afraid, and he'd let that rule him. He was *still* afraid, but it was time to be proactive if he could.

Camden might say no. He probably *should* say no, because marrying Toby could complicate things as much as it could help.

Toby didn't think he would, though. Camden had tried to get closer to Toby while also giving him the space and time he needed. He wanted Toby in his life, and while Toby was still wary, he was starting to think that he wanted Camden in his life, too.

"We can't fight. There aren't enough of us who would know what to do, and while most of the pack is behind you on this, I don't think we can sacrifice them," Griffin said.

Camden rubbed his face. He felt like he hadn't slept in a week, and maybe he hadn't, since it had been almost that long since the Springfield envoy had visited. "I don't *want* the pack to fight." He knew as well as Griffin that the pack members weren't fighters.

A few of them had been in the military, and one was a police officer, but everyone else would be helpless. Camden couldn't ask them to fight. He didn't *want* to ask them to fight. They'd get hurt, and that would go against everything his father had taught him about being an alpha.

"What are we going to do, then? The Springfield pack hasn't pushed yet, but their envoy is still here, and it's almost been a week. They're not going to wait forever."

"I know."

Griffin sighed. "I know you can't choose."

"Choose?"

"Between Toby and Sam. One is your mate. The other is Frederic's."

"I'm not about to *sell* either of them. I wouldn't even if they weren't anyone's mates. I wouldn't even if they weren't pack members, which they are. My father wouldn't have allowed any of us to be taken, and I won't, either."

"That doesn't leave you a lot of options."

"I know. But I wouldn't be a good alpha if I sold off my pack members."

To Camden's surprise, Griffin smiled. "Your father would be proud of you."

Camden snorted. "For what? Putting the pack in danger?"

"No, although I can't deny we all are. But he'd be proud of you for having your convictions and not giving in to pressure, for protecting the pack and its members, *all* its members, even the newer ones. Most people would have cracked under the pressure, yet here you are, still trying to find a way to keep everyone safe. You're a good alpha, Camden. Your age doesn't matter, not anymore."

Camden smiled. "Thank you." He didn't usually enjoy compliments, but this was different. Griffin was saying he was a good alpha and considering who he was, Camden had needed it. "That makes me feel better, but it doesn't solve our problem."

"You're right, it doesn't. Have you contacted everyone?"

"Yes." Camden tapped his fingertips on his desk. "Terrence said he'd get back to me, so I'm hoping he's going to be able to help."

"Do you think he's going to send us a few of his bears?"

Terrence was the alpha of a sleuth that lived about an hour away from Rosewood. The sleuth lived in a more densely populated area, with more shifters living close by, so it had guards and people to defend its members. Camden wasn't sure Terrence could make do without any of his men, but he was hoping to at least get them for a while, just the time for the Springfield pack to back off. It might not solve the problem in the long run, but it would give them more time to find a definitive solution. Terrence was a friend, and he was sympathetic to Camden's position, even though he hadn't met his mate yet. He'd promised he'd do whatever he could, and Camden believed him.

He hoped it would be enough.

A knock on the door made both him and Griffin look. It was late, and the wind howled outside, reminding Camden of the wolf he was. It had been too long since he'd had the time to have a good run, and he doubted that would change for a while yet.

"I'm going to go see who it is," Griffin said, getting up.

"You should go home once you have. I'm sure your wife isn't happy with me for keeping you here until late every night."

"You're right, she's not, but she understands."

Griffin patted Camden's shoulder before leaving. Camden sighed heavily and let his shoulders droop. He always tried to show strength and assurance when he was with other people, although he suspected Griffin saw right through him. He'd seen Camden grow up, so he knew him well, perhaps better than most in the pack. He knew how hard this was hitting Camden, and he was one of the few in front of whom Camden knew he could show weakness. He still tried not to. He was the alpha, and the fact that Griffin was almost twice his age and had seen him in diapers didn't count.

"Camden?"

Camden blinked at the sound of Toby's voice. "Yes?"

This wasn't what he'd expected. He'd thought his mother

might have come to talk to him, or his brother, or even Leslie, who wasn't happy at being left out of the nightly meeting between Griffin and Camden. But Camden needed her out there to check on the pack and to make sure no one was going to do something stupid like try to sell Toby or Sam before the Springfield pack intervened.

Toby stepped into the room. "Griffin said he was leaving."

"I know. I told him to." Camden hauled himself out of his chair. He felt like he was eighty, or maybe like his body weighed much more than usual. It was the weight of the responsibilities and the worries, but he'd keep on shouldering them. He had to. "Did you need anything?"

Toby shuffled. He looked nervous, but then, he usually did when he was with Camden. Camden wished he didn't, but nothing but time would cure him of that.

"I wanted to talk to you," Toby said.

Camden hoped it wasn't about what was happening with the Springfield pack, because it was all there was on his mind right now, but he knew Toby was as worried as he was— probably more so, actually, though for different reasons.

"Do you want to sit down?" he asked, gesturing at the chairs at his desk.

"I don't know. I was talking with Sam, and he suggested something, but I don't . . ."

Camden smiled. "Whatever he suggested, I'm ready to hear it. I can use the help."

Toby grimaced. "Still that bad, huh?"

"Pretty much. I might have found someone who can help, but I don't know how much. We can still run, you and I, although I'm keeping that as a last resort."

"I don't want to run." Toby straightened his back. "I don't want Sam to run. This is his home. He needs to stay with the pack." He hesitated. "And I *want* to stay with the pack."

That was news to Camden. He'd thought Toby was still

hesitant. He knew Toby wouldn't think twice about leaving if it meant keeping Sam safe, but the fact that he wanted to stay if he could choose made Camden hope that he was getting through to his mate. "What did Sam think we could do?" he didn't want to bring attention to what Toby had said in case Toby regretted it already.

"He—you really aren't planning to sell one of us? Or to ask one of us to sacrifice ourselves?"

"Of course not." Camden would repeat that until Toby believed it. He didn't care how long it took, how many times he had to say the same words.

"Even though it's putting the pack in danger?"

"I'm trying to find a way to keep us all safe. If that doesn't work—"

"You'll run away with me."

"Yes. If it's the only option, I will. I hope it won't come to that, of course." He didn't want to take Toby away from the home he was creating for himself with Sam and their friends, but if that was what was needed to keep him safe, he would.

Toby nodded. "All right. Sam suggested we could get married. Him and Frederic, too. That way, he and I will have one more anchor with the pack, and it will be more difficult for the envoy to try to take us."

Camden had thought about that option, too, of course, but he'd dismissed it. He hadn't thought Toby would want it. He barely talked to Camden, so a marriage had to be far from his mind.

Except it clearly wasn't.

Camden wasn't sure it would work, but Sam hadn't been wrong by thinking it might help. Being married to two members of the Rosewood pack would help keep Toby and Sam safe. It would give the Springfield pack pause because they'd have to find a way around it. They could decide to say fuck it and attack, take Sam and Toby away without caring about the rest, but the other packs wouldn't allow that.

The main reason shifters were able to coexist with humans, albeit uneasily, was because they showed them their human side. Massacring an entire pack to get two unicorn shifters would shatter that illusion. The packs and other shifter groups were at peace, and none of them wanted war.

They'd take care of the Springfield pack if they stepped out of line, but at what cost to Camden and his people?

Camden was going to say no, wasn't he? It would make sense. Why would he want to marry Toby when Toby had barely even talked to him? Toby should have given him a chance. He'd wanted to, but he'd let fear rule him and his decisions, and now they were in this mess, and it was his fault.

"Yes."

Toby blinked. "What?"

Camden seemed hesitant, but not angry. "Yes. To your proposal. Although I'm not sure that telling me your brother thinks we should get married is a proposal. Still, my answer is yes."

Toby wasn't sure what to say. He'd come here hoping Camden would say *yes* but expecting a *no,* and that wasn't what he'd gotten. What now, then?

"But I'd like to know something," Camden continued.

Toby should have known there would be a *but.* "What?"

"Are you doing it only because you want to try to save yourself and your brother?"

"I'm not sure what you mean," Toby said, trying to waste time. If he was honest with himself, he wasn't sure why he was doing it. Yes, there was a part of him that hoped it would be enough to keep both him and Sam—and the pack—safe, but there was more to it. If only Toby's feelings weren't as complicated as they were, he might be able to put them into words.

"You don't like me."

Toby frowned. "Why do you think that?"

"Why shouldn't I? I know you're still wary and afraid, and I understand that. It's one of the reasons I gave you space and time. I didn't want to push you too much. But you haven't tried to talk to me. You haven't tried to get to know me. I was sure you'd decided you didn't want me in your life."

"You're my mate," Toby murmured.

"I am, but it doesn't mean much, does it? It won't change anything if you decide to leave. I know you're staying with us mostly because you want to be with your brother. The fact that we're mates might influence others, but it's obvious it hasn't influenced you, and it's not a bad thing, or a good one. I'm not trying to make you out to be an asshole or anything. I do wish we were closer or that you were open to being with me, but I won't hold it against you if you aren't."

"How could you not?" Toby's parents had been mates, as well as married, and they'd been happy. Toby remembered that well, and yes, he wanted the same with Camden. The main reason he hadn't tried to get close to Camden yet was that he didn't know if he could trust him. They'd only known each other for a few weeks. If it had been longer, Toby knew he'd have relaxed and let go of that fear. He did believe his brother when Sam said that Camden and the others in the pack were good people but believing it and *feeling* it were two different things. There wasn't much he could do to force his brain and his heart to trust someone.

But they didn't have time. They wouldn't if the Springfield pack had what it wanted.

"Why don't you sit down," Camden said, gentle and soft.

This time, Toby did. He sat on one of the chairs and raked a hand through his hair. This was a mess, and he didn't know how to get out of it. He knew Camden would marry him even if he told him he didn't like him. He'd do it because he wanted to save the pack, Sam, and Toby.

But Toby *did* like Camden. He seemed like a good man considering what he was ready to do for someone he barely knew. He had honor. He was compassionate. He was loving and caring. Toby would fall in love with him, in time, and maybe the wedding would give them that time. It might be their only chance at it.

Toby looked at Camden. "I never said I didn't like you. I'm . . . wary of trusting you, that's true. But you can't blame me, not with what I've been through. I've never trusted anyone who wasn't related to me. I never had a reason to. And now I do, and I see how hard you're working for Sam and me, and your pack, and I *want* to trust you. I want to have the time to learn how to do that."

Camden came to crouch in front of Toby. He wasn't touching Toby, and for some reason, Toby wanted him to. He didn't move, though. He was afraid to move. It felt like the smallest mistake might shatter the moment and its promises, and he didn't want to risk that.

He swallowed instead. "I'm *terrified*. I want to trust you, and from everything I've seen, I should, but there's something, a voice in the back of my head, screaming at me that you'll use me if I do. That you only want me for my healing powers. I can *see* you don't and that you have a good heart, but having a good heart doesn't mean you don't make mistakes. And that you can't do bad things, just that you might do them for reasons you think are right."

"Do you think that marrying me might help you with that?" Camden asked.

"How?"

"Well, you already know in your head I wouldn't use either you or your brother. But you can't believe that in your heart yet. But would you believe that I wouldn't use my husband that way? That I wouldn't let anyone take my husband or buy him? Hurt him in any way? I've been doing everything I can to save both you and the pack, and that won't change if we get married. But maybe having that ceremony will help you see that the bond between us is there, that it's real and that I'm not going to renege on it. It might help you have more faith in me."

"There's still divorce."

Camden chuckled and gently touched Toby's knee. "You're right. Not that it changes anything from my point of view, but there is, should you ever want to leave me. And I can't promise you won't. I'm sure living with me won't be a walk in the park. I work too much, and I tend to put the pack before everything else. I'm insecure, and I snap when people notice it. I have a lot of defects that will bother you, and I'm sure the same will go for you. That doesn't mean we can't be happy together, though. There's a reason we're soul mates. We might not *have* to be together, but that bond is a sign we should, or at least I think so."

Toby wanted everything Camden was talking about, even the bad stuff, the snapping, and the too much work. He wanted a family, a place where he'd belong, with people who didn't expect anything from him but love and the stuff people in a relationship expected. He wasn't sure he could do that— he'd never had to, had never had the opportunity to do it— but he wanted to try. And if this meant the Springfield pack would stay away from him and Sam, then he didn't have a reason to step back, did he? Especially since he'd been the one who had proposed to Camden, albeit in a rude, weird way.

It looked like even though they were different, he and Camden wanted the same thing. Maybe not for the same reasons, although would that matter? They both wanted Toby, Sam, and the pack to be safe. They both wanted to try to get to know each other and be together. Was that a bad beginning for a marriage?

Toby swallowed and slid to his knee on the floor. Camden's eyes widened, but he stayed where he was. He was taller, but since he was still crouching, Toby didn't have trouble looking him in the eyes as he asked, "Camden Cook, will you marry me?"

Camden had been smiling before, but it had been a gentle, soft smile. Now it widened into a delighted one—one Toby was stunned to have put on Camden's face. Camden was over the moon about this, wasn't he? He really wanted to marry Toby.

Toby rubbed the back of his head. "I know I don't have a ring, but—"

"Shut up, Toby."

Toby snapped his mouth shut. Camden was still beaming, and Toby wasn't surprised when he said, "My answer is *yes*, like it was earlier. You don't have to say anything to convince me, and I don't need a ring, although I wouldn't mind seeing mine on your finger. I'll marry you, Toby."

He reached out hesitantly, and when Toby realized what he was doing, he leaned closer. Their lips brushed together, and Toby tensed, but Camden didn't push. He moved back instead, still smiling.

"I guess I shouldn't have sent Griffin home," Camden said.

Toby blinked. "What?"

"Who do you think officiates the ceremony when an alpha gets married?"

Camden was certain they should wait a while longer, maybe talk things out once they'd both had the time to think things over, but he couldn't stop thinking about marrying Toby now that Toby had asked him—not once, but twice. Camden hoped Toby wouldn't change his mind, especially since he hadn't asked out of love.

That didn't matter to Camden. He wished Toby loved him, of course, but they'd only known each other for a few weeks, and they hadn't talked much. Toby needed safety and security much more than he needed love right now, and that was okay. Camden hoped they would fall in love with time, once the danger that came with the Springfield pack was gone, but if they didn't, or if only he did, he wouldn't keep Toby in a marriage that didn't make him happy.

All of that wasn't something he needed to think about now, though. No, now he had to think about where he was going to get two rings that fit them, to get Griffin back to his house, and probably Sam, Frederic, Reece, and Sage, too. They'd never forgive Camden if he didn't let them know he and Toby were getting married.

"You want to do this now?" Toby asked, his eyes wide.

"Would you rather wait? Because we can do that." Camden had to remind himself that they were doing it for Toby's safety and not because they were in love. It would be too easy for him to delude himself and let the situation take over. That was the last thing both him and Toby needed right now. Camden had to keep his head level and focus on the Springfield pack and the danger they represented.

And thinking about danger, he should probably let his mom know, too. She'd call Vicky and Bry, but maybe Griffin would manage to come back fast enough that they wouldn't come to the wedding.

Oh, who was he kidding? Of course they'd be there. His mom would have his head otherwise, and she'd display it as a trophy over her fireplace.

Toby shook his head. "I suppose waiting won't make a difference. We don't have rings, though."

He seemed keen on having rings, on putting a visible sign of their union on both of them. The thought shouldn't have thrilled Camden as much as it did. "I'll find rings." Even if he had to make them out of napkin holders or something.

"Are you sure you want to do this? Because —"

Camden took Toby's hand. "I'm sure. You asked me twice, and I said yes both times. Don't second-guess this, Toby. You don't have a reason to. I'm not going to use the fact that we're married against you. I hope you know that by now, and if you don't, well, you'll find out soon enough. But know that even when we're married, you'll be able to leave this house, move back with your brother, or even not move in with me at all if that's what you want." Camden didn't want to assume, especially not when it came to Toby. He was afraid every time he said something, because he didn't know what would make Toby freak out and run.

Toby swallowed, his Adam's apple bobbing. "I'll move in. I should, right? If we're going to be married."

"I doubt anyone will think we're doing it because we're in love, so it wouldn't matter. You can stay with Sam and Frederic if you want. I told you, you're the one who holds all the cards. I'll wait for you to make a move before doing anything."

"I don't feel like it's fair."

"Maybe not, but since I don't have a problem with it, why should you? Do you want to do it right now, then? Should I call Griffin, or should we wait?"

"I want to do it now."

Camden wasn't surprised. Toby wanted to get married to keep himself and his brother safe, so it didn't make sense to wait. "All right. Why don't you call your brother? He's going to want to be here. You can tell him to tell Sage. I don't know about you, but I don't want that many people here, since we have nothing organized. We can have a bigger celebration with the rest of the pack later on, but tonight, I think we should stick to my mother and my siblings if they want to come, Griffin, of course, and Sam, Frederic, Sage, and Reece. Anyone else?"

Toby shook his head. "It's fine. I'll call Sam then?"

"You do that, and I'll call Griffin and my mother."

Camden was only mildly surprised that it took him and Toby only half an hour to get everyone to his house. His mom was shooting arrows with her eyes, but she didn't say anything, and she was there, which was more than Camden had hoped for. She might not be happy about the wedding, but she wouldn't oppose it.

"Are you sure about this?" Griffin asked for what had to be the tenth time.

"I am. I already told you."

The rest of their group, minus Camden's mom who was still glaring daggers at him and Toby, who was in Camden's bedroom freshening up, was moving around the living room. There wasn't much they could do to make this look like a real wedding ceremony, but they were trying.

Sage had brought a bunch of flowers from his garden, and he and Reece were doing the most with them, decorating the room and the fireplace in front of which Toby and Camden would stand when they said their vows. Sam and Frederic were setting up candles, while Bryon was lining up chairs for the witnesses. Vicky couldn't be there because one of her kids had a fever, but she'd tasked Bry to video the ceremony and send it to her.

"There has to be another way," Griffin muttered.

Camden wasn't offended, because he knew he was looking out for him. "Maybe there is, but it doesn't matter. I *want* to do this, and so does Toby. I hope we'll eventually fall in love, but if we don't, well, it's something we can revisit once the Springfield pack is a memory."

"You're the alpha, I guess, and the guy getting married."

"You'll do it?"

"Of course I will. And I hope you two *will* fall in love. I just don't want you to get hurt. I watched you grow up, and while you're not my son, you might as well be."

Camden's chest squeezed. His father would have been the one conducting the ceremony if he'd still been alive, but Griffin was a good substitute. That didn't lessen the pain, but Camden had known for five years that his dad wouldn't be there, and marrying Toby, of all people, helped lessen the sting his absence was creating.

"Ready?" Griffin asked the room. Sam disappeared to grab his brother while Griffin and Camden settled in front of the fireplace, and everyone else sat down. Camden rubbed his hands on his thighs, more nervous than he'd thought he would be. This wasn't a marriage of love yet, but Toby was his mate, his other half, and even without love, it meant something. Camden would never find another person as well-suited to him as Toby was, and hopefully, Toby would eventually realize that.

Sam cleared his throat, and everyone turned to watch him and Toby walk in. Toby was clutching his brother's arm as he looked around, but he was resolute as he walked toward Camden, and Camden stood straighter.

Whatever the reason they were getting married, they were doing the right thing, and he was proud of that.

"Now, as everyone here knows, this wedding is a bit rushed. If Toby was a woman, I'd ask him if we'll get a surprise in eight months, but I'll keep my mouth shut," Griffin said. "Let's get straight to the point, shall we?" He looked at Camden. "Camden, we all know what your answer will be, but do you take Toby as your husband, for better and for worse, and all that?"

Camden wished he and Toby had had the time to write their vows, or at least to think about them but this would do. Maybe they could have a longer and more formal ceremony later on. Right now, even though Griffin was rushing through things, this was perfect.

"I do." Griffin hadn't been wrong when he'd said that everyone knew Camden's answer.

Griffin nodded and looked at Toby. "Same for you, son. Do you take Camden here as your husband?"

Camden held his breath. It felt like everyone in the room was doing the same thing as they stared at Toby and waited for him to say it.

Toby licked his lips. "I do."

The weight on Camden's chest lifted. He beamed at Toby, and Toby smiled back at him, more hesitantly, but so very real.

"Then, with the powers given me as the beta of this pack, I declare you husband and husband. I don't know if you want to kiss, but feel free to do it if you do."

Camden hadn't thought that far, so he stayed right where he was, but to his surprise, Toby leaned closer and pressed their lips together.

Then he said, "I'm still waiting for my ring, you know," and Camden burst out laughing.

CHAPTER FIVE

Toby couldn't sleep. He wasn't sure why—the bed was comfortable, his door was locked, so he was sure no one could sneak in while he was sleeping, and he'd eaten well last night. He and Camden, along with their friends, had celebrated their wedding, and Toby still couldn't quite wrap his mind around that.

He raised his hand and peered at the ring on his finger in the darkness. He had no idea where Camden had found them, but after everyone had left last night, he'd knocked on the door of the guest bedroom he'd given Toby. He'd asked Toby to give him his hand, and when Toby had, he'd slipped the ring on his finger. Toby had been too shocked to ask about it, but now it was four in the morning, and even though he'd only slept fitfully, he couldn't go back to sleep. He couldn't stop thinking.

He sighed and dropped his hand, looking at the door instead. Camden was only one door down in the hallway, and for some reason, Toby wanted to go to him. He wanted to talk, to find out how Camden looked first thing in the morning with his hair all messed up and his eyes still sleepy.

And he could, couldn't he? He hadn't moved his meager belongings yet, but he knew Camden wanted him to, and he was going to do it. He and Camden were married, and while Toby still wasn't a hundred percent sure of anything but Sam in his life, he knew that was important to Camden and that he wouldn't betray their vows. He wasn't going to give Toby away.

He was going to love him instead.

Toby pushed the blankets away. He had no idea what he was doing and what he was going to find, but he wasn't going to find out if he stayed in bed. He could go to the kitchen and make some coffee if he chickened out, but he and Camden were married, and that meant that Camden was supposed to be there for him when he couldn't sleep and comfort him, right? Toby hoped Camden wouldn't expect anything from him. He was about to sneak into his bed after all, or at least, he was going to try.

The floor creaked under Toby's feet when he stepped into the hallway. He paused and peered at Camden's door. It wasn't closed all the way, but Toby couldn't see anything through the opening, not from where he was.

He snuck closer and gently pushed the door open.

"Toby? Is everything okay?"

Toby's heart almost jumped out of his chest at the sound of Camden's voice. "I didn't realize you were awake," he answered in a strangled tone.

"I didn't mean to scare you. I sleep very lightly, so I heard you leave your bedroom. Is everything okay?"

Toby's heart was still racing, but he didn't want Camden to think he was afraid of him. "I'm fine. I just didn't expect this."

"What did you expect?" Camden's voice was gentle, and it gave Toby the courage to step into his bedroom.

"I can't sleep anymore."

"Worried?"

Now that he was inside, Toby could see Camden sitting up on his bed. The curtains were drawn, but that didn't mean Toby missed the fact that Camden liked to sleep shirtless, even though the air in the room was chilly. "In part. I didn't expect all of this to happen. The wedding, spending the night . . ." Toby twisted the ring around his finger. He wasn't used to it yet. That would take a while.

"You would have felt better if you'd gone home."

But Toby had insisted he wanted to stay with Camden. Camden was his husband now, even though they weren't a couple. "I wanted to be here."

"Is there anything I can do for you?"

That was the question, wasn't it? Toby wasn't even sure why he'd decided to go to Camden's room. "I didn't want to be alone." That felt like the best answer.

"Do you want to climb in? To sleep, of course. I don't expect anything from you other than that. I'm not sure how comfortable you'll be, but—"

"Yes, thank you." Toby moved before he could talk himself into going back to his bedroom to look at the ceiling for a few more hours.

He couldn't see Camden's expression, but Camden raised the blanket, and Toby slipped under it. He stretched out on his back and waited to see what was going to happen. Camden stayed true to his word and kept to his side of the bed, even though he turned to face Toby.

Toby had no idea what to do. Every fiber of his being yearned to move closer to Camden, so he did, inch by inch, sliding toward the middle of the bed.

"What do you need?" Camden asked, his voice slightly rougher than before.

"Can you . . . hold me?" Toby wanted to feel less alone, and in his heart, he knew Camden wouldn't take advantage of that.

"Of course. You only have to ask. Come here."

Toby slid the rest of the way and slotted himself against Camden's body. Camden was warm and hard, and exactly what Toby had wanted. He made Toby feel like he was where he belonged—and maybe he was. He could think that out tomorrow, though.

For now, he slept

The pounding on the door woke him up. He was disoriented for a moment, not remembering where he was, but Camden was already getting out of bed, and as Toby watched him leave the bedroom, he realized he'd spent the last hours of the night sleeping in his mate's arms. He wasn't sure what to do about that, but he'd have time to think things over later. Whoever was at the door needed them to open now.

Toby rolled out of bed and followed Camden downstairs. Camden was already opening the door, and Toby's stomach sank when he saw Griffin and Leslie on the other side of it.

"What happened?" Camden asked.

He and Toby already knew, though. It was easy to guess.

"The envoy is back."

Camden rubbed his face. "Shit. Give me fifteen minutes. Take him to my office. I'll be right there."

"I'll make coffee," Leslie said, pushing past Griffin.

Toby went back to his bedroom. Camden wasn't going to face the envoy alone this time. Toby was still terrified, but they were married, and that made him the alpha's husband. They were supposed to work together, especially in this case since Toby was involved.

Camden seemed surprised to see him waiting for him when he left his bedroom, his hair damp and dressed. "You don't have to come. I promise you I won't accept whatever deal he thinks I'll have to take. This is your home, Toby, and Sam's."

"I know. I want to be with you when you see him, if that's okay."

"Of course it is." Toby might be imagining it, but he thought he saw respect in Camden's eyes. He hoped he had. He wanted his mate to respect him and to know that he could help. They were in this together, whether Toby wanted it or not, and he'd honor that.

Camden stopped before opening the door to his office. He took Toby's hand, looked at him — possibly to make sure Toby was okay with it — and when Toby nodded, he strode in. Toby kept up with him and tried not to stare at the man sitting in front to the desk. Camden dragged Toby on the other side of it and gently pushed him into the chair he no doubt used every day.

"Good morning. My apologies for making you wait, but I'm sure you'll understand that as newlyweds, we wanted some time alone to enjoy our new status."

The man arched a brow. "Newlywed. I assume this boy is one of the unicorns?"

Toby bristled but kept his mouth shut. He had no idea how this worked, and he didn't want Camden to have trouble only because he'd been offended.

"Toby is a man, and yes, he's one of the unicorn shifters and my mate."

"I see. We'll take the other one, then."

"I already told you that no member of my pack is for sale. If Sam chooses to move in with the Springfield pack, I won't have a problem with it, but he didn't seem inclined to do that when I talked to him, and neither was his mate. This is their home, and what they are doesn't matter."

"Oh, it does. And you have two more days to convince him that moving will be the best outcome for everyone involved." The envoy smirked. "My alpha expected me back today, but I'm sure he won't mind me giving you an extra two days to celebrate your marriage."

They were in fucking trouble.

Griffin had led the envoy out, leaving Toby and Camden alone in Camden's office. The ultimatum hung above their heads, and Camden had no idea what to do. He'd saved Toby by marrying him, but now Sam was in danger, and there was no way out of that. Camden couldn't marry Sam, and even if Frederic and Sam got married, it wouldn't stop the Springfield pack. They'd demand that both of them move, something that wasn't going to happen, no matter how horrifying the alternatives were. Camden would sooner help them run away than hand them over.

Camden needed to call Terrence again. He'd promised to send people to help, but Camden hadn't heard from him again, and now he needed that help more than ever.

"What are we going to do?" Toby asked. He sounded defeated, and Camden hated it. He hated that this was what he was giving Toby on their first day as married men.

"I'm going to call Terrence again. He promised me he'd help, and we need him to." If he couldn't do anything, well, Camden supposed he should start looking into how much tickets to Canada would cost. Frederic and Sam needed to be as far away as possible from the pack by the time the envoy came back. Possibly, Toby, too. Camden wasn't sure he wanted to take the risk of having him here when the envoy realized what had happened, just in case the man was an idiot as well as ruthless and an asshole.

Toby sat in the chair vacated by the envoy and watched as Camden made his phone call. His presence was soothing, and Camden couldn't imagine what his life would be like if he had to send Toby away. They hadn't shared much until now, but having Toby there felt right, more than anything else Camden had ever done.

"Cam. I was about to call you," Terrence said when he answered.

The knot in Camden's chest relaxed. "Please tell me it's because you have good news for me. The envoy came back, and he's going to take Sam in two days if I don't find a way to stop him."

"Not Toby? I suppose it makes sense since he's your mate, even though you're not together."

"We're married, as of last night."

"Yeah? Congrats, man, and yes, I do have good news. I already sent someone your way. They should be there tomorrow."

"They?" That sounded good. More than one person was exactly what they needed. A small army, possibly.

"The Smith twins."

Twins? "Only two of them?"

Terrence sighed. "I'm sorry I can't do more, but I promise you, they'll be enough."

"I don't know, Terrence. We're facing the Springfield pack."

"And those two have faced bigger packs. Trust me, Cam. I wouldn't send them off if I didn't think they could help. Hell, I'd have rather kept them here, but they never stay in the same place for long."

"They're not sleuth members?"

"No. They were passing through the town and asked if I wanted to hire them for a bit. That's how I know they're good at what they do. They taught my men to fight and to defend the sleuth. They helped us a few months ago, when the pride next door tried to encroach on our territory."

"And you don't mind parting with them?" If they were as good as Terrence was making it sound, Camden wasn't sure why he was sending them his way.

"They were telling me they were planning to leave soon. I told you they never stay for long in one place. They don't have a family except for each other. They're wanderers, and it'll make sense to you when you meet them."

Camden trusted Terrence. He wouldn't have asked for his help otherwise. He trusted all the alphas he'd called, but

Terrence wasn't just an alpha. He and Camden had built up a relationship over the years, and Camden considered him a friend instead of merely another alpha. "All right. Thank you." Camden wasn't sure what two men could do against another pack, but he supposed he'd find out soon enough.

"You got married, huh?"

"Yeah. We wanted to make sure Toby wouldn't be taken away, but now Springfield is talking about taking Sam."

"You know that your life would be much easier if you gave in."

"I know. That doesn't mean I will. Sam and Toby are just as free as me and you. They're human beings. What they can do and what they can shift into doesn't change that. I might only be a wolf, and you might only be a bear, but the fact that we deserve to be free and to make our own decisions wouldn't change even if we were unicorns."

"You have a knack for picking up strays, Cam."

"Sage isn't a stray, and neither are Sam and Toby."

"I' suppose they're not, not anymore. I can't even begin to imagine you married."

"It'll happen to you sooner or later."

Terrence barked out a laugh. "Probably. From the way the women in the sleuth are harping about me getting married, you'd think I was seventy and about to give my last breath."

"The heir thing, huh?"

"Yeah. How did you get around that? I remember that your mom was pushing for grandkids."

"Toby and I can have children if we want." Camden looked at Toby when he said that, so he didn't miss Toby's wide eyes and his gaping mouth. "Once this is over and we have time to talk about it, of course. We're going to take our relationship slowly."

"Getting married doesn't sound like you're going slow."

"We had to do that."

"I get it. Do you regret it?"

Camden looked at Toby again. Even if the only thing he got from their marriage was to keep Toby safe, it would have been worth it. *Toby* was worth it and being married to him was far from being a sacrifice, even if they ended up only being friends. "No. I don't think I ever will."

"Well, better you than me. Let me know how the twins work out, okay?"

"You can assume they didn't if you don't hear from me."

"Stop that. You make it sound desperate, and only death is desperate."

"Don't get all philosophical on me now."

Toby was still watching Camden when Camden hung up, so he tried to reassure him. "He's sending someone. They'll get here tomorrow, so in time for us to face the envoy again."

Toby nodded, but that wasn't what he asked when he opened his mouth. "Your friend asked you if you regretted marrying me?"

"You heard?"

"Not well, but your side of the conversation was enough for me to take a guess."

"He did, yes. The last time we talked, I told him you and I weren't spending time together, which considering what's happening, is normal. We had too much to worry about to date or whatever."

"And now you find yourself married to me. Are you sure you don't regret it?"

"I'm sure."

Toby rose from the chair. He was hesitant, and Camden didn't move. He watched him walk around the desk and come closer. He realized he was holding his breath when Toby touched his arm and he let it out.

Camden's eyebrows shot up when Toby slowly sat in his lap. "What are you doing?" he asked. He sounded breathless already, and Toby hadn't even done anything. Hell, Camden didn't know if he was *planning* to do anything except using him as a chair, which was perfectly all right with him.

Toby wrapped his arms around Camden's neck. "I know we haven't started off well, and that it was my fault."

Camden put his arms around Toby's hips. He made sure to keep his hold loose so that Toby could leave if he wanted to, but damn, he hoped Toby wouldn't want to. "It was no one's fault. The situation hasn't exactly been easy. You spent four years as a prisoner, and now that you're free, there are people trying to make you one again. I understand, Toby, and as I already told you, I don't expect anything from you. I promise."

"I know. That's one of the reasons I asked you to marry me. I'm starting to believe that I can have all of this."

"All of this?" Camden didn't want to let himself hope, but he should, right? Toby was saying the right things, and he was sitting in his lap.

"The pack. A family." Toby paused. "You. You really only want me to be happy."

"I do." And Camden was ready to do anything to make that happen.

Toby's mind was still reeling from his short conversation with Camden—and from the courage he'd had to sit in Camden's lap as they talked. He'd wanted to kiss Camden, but he wasn't that brave, not yet. He knew that if things went wrong, he'd have to leave, and he didn't want his heart to break because of what he was leaving behind. Being able to let go of his distrust was opening a new future for him, a future in which he'd have a husband and a family, but the danger was still there, and Camden would send him and Sam away if that was what was needed.

Which was why Toby had decided to talk to Sam.

Camden had decided to hold a pack meeting later that day to tell them about the situation with the Springfield pack and that he and Toby had gotten married. Toby knew not everyone was going to be happy. A few of the older members didn't see him with a good eye. Camden had explained it was because they didn't like the fact that he wouldn't be having an heir with his wife like all the other alphas had done before him. They didn't want things to change, to evolve, and Toby thought that was stupid. He and Camden were soul mates. They were married.

Things *were* going to change.

"Toby," Sam said. He was beaming. "How was your first night as a married man?"

Toby wasn't sure how to tell him they were still in trouble, and that the trouble had found them already this morning. "It was okay." It had been more than okay when he'd slept in Camden's bed, but the rest of the morning was pretty much a nightmare, at least until the Springfield envoy had left.

"Okay?" Sam frowned. "Wait. Did something happen? Please tell me Camden didn't hurt you or force you —"

"No, of course not. I spent the night in my bed. But the Springfield envoy came around this morning."

Sam paled. "Shit."

"Pretty much, yeah. Can I come in?"

"Of course. Frederic already left, but I'll text him to let him know."

"Maybe you should ask him to come home."

"Maybe. He'll probably come back anyway. He didn't want to go, to begin with. He's worried I'll disappear if he's not with me. He even called Naila to ask her if it would be okay with her if I stayed home for a bit."

"How did you take that?"

Sam grimaced. "Not well, even though I understand why

he's doing it. He's terrified, and so am I, but I don't want to give up the life I'm building. Besides, Naila's house is probably safer than this one. She lives hidden in the forest, and I doubt that anyone other than the pack members know where exactly. The Springfield pack could probably find out, but not before we'd realize what was happening."

"Fear isn't rational, though. Frederic probably needs to do everything he can to keep you safe, and he's not overthinking what that means for you, not as long as he's sure you're okay."

"The same goes for Camden and you, right?"

Toby shrugged. "I guess." He was trying to keep things light, but he knew the truth now. Camden was ready to do anything for him, even renounce to having him in his life. That thought made Toby feel confused and humble, and he wasn't sure how to deal with it.

They settled in the kitchen, and Sam made some hot chocolate. Toby wasn't thirsty, but it was better to hold it and warm his hands than to keep fiddling with everything he could reach. He was nervous, and nothing would change that until he knew both he and his brother were safe.

"What's going to happen now?" Sam asked. "I suppose Camden told the envoy that the two of you are married."

"He did."

"And what did the envoy say?"

Toby sighed. "That he'd take you instead. We have two days to convince you to go."

Sam's hands tightened around his mug, but he didn't yell at Toby. He nodded. "I see."

"Camden isn't going to agree."

"I know."

"The envoy mentioned that you and Frederic could both move."

"Frederic isn't going to want to. *I* don't want to."

"We'll fight, then."

"The pack can't win. I've been asking around, and the Springfield pack is much bigger than us. They're going to crush us if we don't give them what they want."

"One of Camden's friends is sending people to help. I don't know how useful they'll be, but from what I heard, Camden's friend thinks they can help."

"Even so. The pack is in danger, and it's my fault."

Toby's stomach twisted. "No, it's not. Everything was okay here until I arrived, and now I've made things worse by marrying Camden." Sam wasn't going anywhere, but maybe Toby would.

He didn't want to. He didn't want to leave his brother and the pack, even though he hadn't been there long. He didn't want to leave Camden and their marriage. But it would be the right thing to do.

Camden and the pack had welcomed him, and he was thanking them by putting them in danger, and for what? For a life he'd only been able to dream about until now. He'd spent four years as a prisoner. Would it be that bad if he spent another four with the Springfield pack? Another five, or ten? He didn't know freedom and what it was like. He'd only had a taste, and while he wanted more of it, he wasn't sure it was worth putting all these people in danger.

"Don't even think about it," Sam snapped.

"What?"

"You are *not* going to live with that pack. I don't have any authority over you, but I'm going to do whatever I have to do to make sure that doesn't happen."

Toby didn't ask him how he knew. It had probably been evident from the conversation and Toby's silence. Sam had always been able to read him anyway, even when they were kids. He'd stopped him from doing enough stupid things. "This is my fault. The Springfield pack is only here because there are two of us. If I hadn't come—"

"Then you'd still be with that gang."

"Maybe so, but at least they never really hurt me. I could have stayed with them."

"And now you want to give yourself up. You don't even know what the pack is planning to do with you."

"Use me for my healing power. It's what everyone always wants."

"But what if they do worse? What if they beat you, things like that? And what about Camden? You're his husband, but even if you weren't, he wouldn't let you sacrifice yourself like this."

"It's because I'm his mate that he doesn't want me to do it, not in spite of it. Sam, if I weren't his mate, he probably would have let me go. He'd have saved his pack instead of me. Many lives for one."

Sam grabbed Toby's hand and squeezed so hard it hurt. "He wouldn't have. Cam is a good man. What the Springfield pack is doing is wrong, and he wouldn't have allowed them to do it even if you hadn't been anything to him. But you *are* something, and that changes things. He's not going to let you do this. He doesn't want to, and neither do I. No *one* wants you to go."

"The rest of the pack—"

"Can go fuck themselves. If things come to that, then the four of us will leave. Don't give up on Camden and what you can have with him because you feel guilty. You're not. The Springfield pack is in the wrong here, not you. Not Camden. Only them. And we'll find a way to get out of this, even if we have to leave. I can't lose you again, Toby. It would break me."

Shit. Toby wanted Sam to be happy. He was between a rock and a hard place—sacrifice his future and his happiness, and possibly Sam's, too, or let the Springfield pack hurt the pack.

"Give those people Camden found the time to get here before making any decisions, okay?" Sam asked. He sounded desperate, as desperate as Toby felt.

"I don't want to go," Toby murmured.

"I know. And you're not going to. I'll go there myself if I have to."

This wasn't Camden's first pack meeting, but it was the one that made him the most nervous, even considering the one he'd organized when his father had died and he'd become the alpha. Everyone had known what was going on then, and the entire pack had supported him through his grief and the learning process of taking his father's place. Today, most pack members weren't aware of who the Springfield pack envoy was, even though they'd seen him twice already. They knew about Toby, but they had no idea he was Camden's mate and that they were married.

Camden was *not* looking forward to this.

He knew not everyone in the pack was going to be happy about what was happening. Hell, no one would be happy, but he'd probably have the support of the youngest members and part of the older guard. His mom would be behind him, of course, but there was no telling about the others. Hopefully, they'd realize that this wasn't about Toby being Camden's mate, but about being good people and not selling human beings.

"You'll be fine," Leslie murmured.

"I sure hope I will."

"We already know who's going to be a problem. It's not great, but it could be worse. Most of the pack will stand with you."

Even though Camden had known that, it was good to hear. He nodded once and stood up, clearing his throat.

They had the meetings at his house, much like they did when his father was alive. He, Griffin, and Leslie were on the porch, while the rest of the pack was on the ground so they could see him. Some of them had brought chairs and blankets to sit, and Camden wondered if it wouldn't be a good idea to build a place to do this rather than have everyone standing in the cold. It was something to think about later, though. Right now, he had to focus on everything else. Toby was in the house with Sam, Frederic, Reece, and Sage, just in case. Camden didn't want him to be there when the first reactions occurred. He knew his pack well enough to be aware those reactions probably wouldn't be good. Angry people tended to be the loudest, and Toby was already torturing himself over this more than enough. He didn't need to hear the stuff some people would have to say.

"I'm sure some of you have noticed the man coming and going in the past week," Camden started.

That got everyone's attention. They looked at him, waiting for him to explain.

He took a deep breath. "He's an envoy from the Springfield pack. He was sent to give us an ultimatum—either we sell Sam or his brother to him, or they'll take one of them by force. And as I'm sure you already suspect, I refused to hand Sam or Toby over."

Noise exploded as everyone tried to talk at the same time. Camden had expected that, so he gave the crowd a few minutes before raising his hands. "Everyone. I know this isn't easy to deal with. Trust me, I've been thinking about it ever since the man first came here. I contacted other alphas, and we're getting help, so you don't have to worry about this." Or at least, Camden hoped they wouldn't have to. He trusted Terrence to know what he was doing and who he was sending them, but he couldn't help but wonder how two men were going to keep the Springfield pack away.

Camden swallowed. "There's something else. When I first met Toby, I knew he was my mate from the first time I smelled him. We got married last night. We'll have a party later on, but—"

Camden's voice was drowned out by the sound of congratulations, surprise, and grumbling. He leaned against the railing and breathed in and out as he tried to assess what the pack thought about this. They hadn't protested when he'd declared that he wasn't handing anyone over to the Springfield pack, but maybe this would change things.

One of the oldest members of the pack, a woman who had to be close to a hundred because she'd already been old when Camden was a kid, raised her hand. The pack didn't have a council of elders like others had, but that didn't mean people didn't respect her and the others. Silence fell on the pack members as they waited for her to speak.

"With all due respect, Alpha Cook," she started, and Camden knew this wasn't going to be good.

"Yes?" he forced himself to say.

"You need an heir. How are you going to have one when your husband is, well, a man?"

At least she wasn't pushing for Camden to send Toby away—yet. "Toby and I haven't talked about it yet, considering the problem with the Springfield pack. The fact that we're both men doesn't mean we can't have children, though."

"Any child born outside your marriage—"

"I wasn't talking about taking a lover. We might adopt."

"But the child wouldn't be yours."

Camden had to resist the urge to roll his eyes. "Not by blood, but any child Toby and I will have, whatever way we have them, will be ours, and will be loved. As I was saying, there's adoption, but also surrogacy. But it's a decision Toby and I will make, no one else."

"And if you *don't* have children?"

That was the crux of the question. The alpha position in this pack had always been hereditary. Camden had become the alpha after his father had died. His father had become the alpha after his own father had died, and while Camden's great-grandfather had stepped down rather than died, his grandfather had become the alpha after him. It was tradition, which was why both Camden's mother and the woman talking now were pushing for heirs.

Camden knew she and some of the others weren't going to like this, but it needed to be said. "I know this pack has always followed tradition when it comes to the alpha position. I don't think that's necessarily a good thing, though. We were lucky that all our recent alphas were good men who kept the good of the pack in mind. I think that the person best suited for the position should have it, even if they're not related to my family." He raised his hands to keep the crowd quiet. "But that's not something we need to discuss now. As I said, the Springfield pack is our most urgent matter right now. Everything else can wait until we've dealt with them. As always, my door is open if any of you want to talk to me. Talk to Griffin or Leslie first, so you don't all end up needing to talk to me on the same day. Thank you for coming."

Camden didn't need to say anything else. He knew the pack had probably a dozen questions for him, but he couldn't answer all of them now, and most pack members would calm down by the time they got to him to talk.

"How did it go?" Frederic asked when Camden stepped in. "It sounded okay from here, except for the heir interrogation."

Camden had to smile at that. "I'm not surprised someone brought it up. It went okay. No one asked that I deliver Toby and Sam to the Springfield pack, so that's good. People are scared and worried, but they're still good people."

Frederic patted Camden's shoulder. "You'll always have

us, though. Remember that."

Camden looked at their little group. Sage was pale and wringing his hands, but he nodded even as he leaned closer to Reece. Reece didn't touch him, but his gaze told Camden that he'd do anything he had to do to protect Sage. Hopefully, that would be nothing. It was Camden's job to protect his pack members, and he was doing his best to do that. He could only hope that his best would be enough.

"Do you need anything?" Sage asked.

"No. Go home, sleep. Rest. The people Terrence sent will be arriving tomorrow, and the envoy from the Springfield pack will be back the day after tomorrow. We need to be ready for all of that, and for what comes next."

They filed out, patting Camden's arm and shoulder, letting him know they were there for him without talking. He closed the door behind them, which left him alone with Toby.

"I thought you might cave in," Toby said.

Camden faced him. "Never. I already told you that."

"You did. I still thought that facing your pack might change things. I'm surprised no one demanded you handed Sam or me off to the Springfield pack."

Camden sighed. "I'm sure some of them thought about it, but they're good people. Some are too attached to old traditions. It doesn't make them bad people, though, and they don't want to sacrifice anyone and compromise the integrity of the pack. But if it comes to it, we'll leave. You and I. We're married. We're soul mates. We're one. We're in this together, whether other people like it or not. That's a promise."

But hopefully, things wouldn't come to that.

CHAPTER SIX

Toby wasn't sure he'd ever get used to waking up in Camden's arms. It was strange, but in a good way.

"Good morning," Camden murmured. He was plastered against Toby's back, his arms around Toby's waist.

He felt like home. He *was* home, no matter how hard Toby had fought it and how insecure he felt. Now he needed the Springfield pack to back the hell off so he could finally start living this new life.

"Good morning," he said, rolling to face Camden.

Camden was always gorgeous, but even more so when he'd just woken up. He looked more vulnerable and softer, and it was hard not to fall in love with him. It was always hard, but when Toby saw him like this, especially so.

He snuggled against Camden's chest. He was aware of the way Camden made sure their groins didn't touch, and while he might be a virgin, he'd seen enough during the four years he'd spent with the gang to know exactly what was going on. Hell, he was a guy. He'd woken up with an erection often enough. He understood why Camden was trying to keep him away—he was so gentle, and he wanted to make sure Toby wasn't confronted by something he wasn't ready for—but he didn't want that kind of protection anymore.

Toby had no idea *what* he was ready for, but he wanted to find out, and that wouldn't happen if Camden didn't give him a chance. They were married, and while Camden didn't have expectations, Toby did. He'd watched how much love there was between his parents, and he wanted that, too. They'd been lucky to find each other. They'd been soul mates like Toby and Camden were, and Toby yearned to have the same kind of relationship with Camden.

He tangled his legs with Camden's and pushed their bodies closer until they were flush against each other from groin to neck.

"Toby—" Camden started, but Toby already knew what he was going to say. He'd caution Toby on continuing this. He'd make sure Toby was okay with it.

Toby was, and he didn't want to talk about it. "Please, Cam?" he murmured.

When Camden didn't move, Toby surged up and kissed him. Camden relaxed and pulled Toby closer. *This* was what Toby had wanted. This was what they were supposed to do, to be.

Camden stopped being cautious.

Toby was a little wary, but he knew Camden wouldn't force him to do anything, that he'd make sure Toby was okay. He'd gotten good at reading Toby's body language, and Toby made sure to stay relaxed as they both pushed the clothes they'd slept in away.

He'd never been naked with anyone. He'd never shared a bed with anyone. It was a first time in more ways than one, and he was glad Camden was the man he was with right now.

Camden's body felt so good against Toby's. He was gentle but firm as he rolled them until Toby was spread under him. He didn't ask Toby if he was okay, and Toby was grateful for that. He didn't want to talk. He wanted to feel.

Camden looked down at Toby. Then he slid down Toby's body. Toby's eyes went wide when he felt his mate's breath on his cock. He knew what Camden was about to do, and he had no idea how to deal with it.

Warm lips closed around his cock. Toby had never felt anything like that. It was warm and wet and tight, and *God*, he was going to come all over Camden's face in about five seconds.

It took longer than that, but not nearly as long as Toby wished it had. He never wanted it to end, but then Camden sucked while also gently stroking between Toby's legs, the inside of his thighs and his balls, darting between Toby's ass cheeks as Toby arched under him.

"Just let go, Toby. I can tell you're resisting, but you don't have to wait for me."

"I want you to feel good," Toby managed to grind out.

"I *am* feeling good." Camden rubbed his cock against Toby's leg. "This is perfectly fine for me. Focus on yourself, okay? I'll take care of everything else."

Toby nodded. It was a relief to know Camden didn't mind. Toby would have the time to take care of him next time. There *would* be a next time—he was sure of that. He couldn't think about this not happening again.

Toby screwed his eyes shut and let go. He could feel Camden moving against him, but like Camden had told him, he focused on himself and his pleasure. It was hard not to with Camden's lips and tongue playing him as if they'd been doing this forever. It felt like he knew exactly what to do to Toby to make him come, and once Toby stopped resisting, it only took Toby seconds to come.

It felt like it lasted forever, and when it was over, Toby couldn't do anything but flop on the mattress and let Camden do whatever he needed to do to make himself come. He wanted to help, but watching Camden take himself in hand and masturbate over him was the hottest thing Toby had ever seen.

"We should probably get up," Camden said about half an hour later. They were still in bed, wrapped around each other, and Toby didn't want to get up.

He wanted this cocoon to last forever. He felt protected and like nothing that happened outside could touch them, even though he knew it wasn't true.

He forced himself to sit up. "I'll go make coffee. You should shower. We don't know when those men your friend sent are going to get here." He kissed Camden's shoulder, and the gesture gave him a little thrill. He could do that any time he wanted now.

Camden smiled and kissed the tip of Toby's nose. "I'll be right there."

Toby went to the kitchen to start the coffee. He was grateful he'd dressed even though he hadn't yet showered when someone knocked on the front door. Toby went to open it, expecting Griffin or Leslie, or maybe even Sam. He wouldn't be surprised if his brother wanted to spend the next few days with him, just in case.

But he didn't recognize the two men standing at the door.

They were tall, way taller than him, and they were identical twins. They both wore leather jackets, but one of them had a bright pink t-shirt under it while the other wore a flannel shirt. The flannel shirt wearer had long, blond-reddish hair, while the other twin's hair was short.

They had to be the men Camden was expecting. "Yes?" Toby asked, proud that his voice shook only a little.

The short-haired twin grinned. "Hey, cutie. I'm Carey, and this is Lennox. Terrence said you guys need help?"

Yep, they were the twins Camden was expecting. Toby stepped aside. "Come in."

"You're not the alpha, right? No offense, because you're cute and all kinds of adorable, but you don't strike me as an alpha."

"That's because I'm not." Toby closed the door behind them and led them to the kitchen. "I'm Toby."

Carey grinned. "Nice to meet you, Toby. Ignore my brother. He never talks much. So, what's your problem?"

"Another pack. Terrence didn't tell you that?"

"He said one of his friends needed us."

"And you came? Without asking questions?"

"It was time for us to move on anyway. What did this pack do to you, then? A cutie like you shouldn't have to worry about this kind of stuff."

Toby rolled his eyes. "Do you want coffee?"

Lennox grunted, and since Toby wasn't sure whether that was a yes or a no, he decided to pour him a cup. He bet Lennox took it black, but instead, he watched with wide eyes as Lennox dropped about half the pot of sugar into it, then added enough milk to make it look like there was barely any coffee in there.

"Yeah, don't mind him. He's a sweetie inside, and he takes his coffee with, well, little coffee," Carey said. He put sugar into his own cup and settled at the counter. "What did this other pack do, then? You can tell me, honey."

"I'd appreciate it if you didn't call my husband honey," Camden drawled from the kitchen door. His hair was still damp, but he was dressed, even though his feet were bare.

Carey groaned. "Your husband? Damn. The cutest ones are always taken."

Camden wasn't sure what to make of the two men sitting in his kitchen. They were the twins Terrence had sent him, and from the little he'd heard before walking into the kitchen, Camden didn't think they were dangerous, not to Toby anyway. He didn't even care that one kept calling Toby pet names. Toby was an adult, and he could deal with that if it bothered him. He looked more amused than anything, though.

"I'm Camden," he said, striding toward the smart ass with the big mouth.

The man smiled. "I'm Carey, the cute twin. This is Lennox."

"Welcome to the Rosewood pack. What did Terrence tell you?"

"Nothing much. Just that you were a good friend of his and that you needed help. Your husband here told us you're dealing with the Springfield pack?"

Camden took the cup of coffee Toby was handing him and kissed his forehead. "Thank you." He turned toward Carey. "We are. They sent an envoy a week or so ago. They made demands we're not ready to fulfill."

"Are you going to tell us what they want? Because it would make it easier. I mean, Terrence said you were a nice guy and we like Terrence, so we don't think he'd lie, but we want to know what we're up against and why."

Camden looked at Toby. He didn't want the word about the two unicorn shifters to go further than it already had. He suspected the Springfield pack was keeping it quiet because they didn't want other shifters to try to get where they were, although he couldn't be sure. He didn't know if he could trust the twins, though, no matter what Terrence thought.

"I'm a unicorn shifter," Toby said.

Carey was still smiling. "Yeah? You're special."

"So is my brother. We both live here. The Springfield pack wants one of us, and they're not taking no for an answer."

"I see. So they're going to take you or your brother, whatever it takes for that to happen."

"Pretty much. Camden has already told them that Sam and I can make our own decisions and that he wasn't going to force either of us to do anything, but the envoy and the pack aren't taking *no* for an answer. Our pack is small, smaller than theirs. There's nothing we can do against them, not if they decide to attack us." He eyed the twins. "I'm not sure you two are going to be enough."

Camden's heart felt like it had swelled when Toby had said *our pack*. He considered himself part of the pack now, and nothing could have made Camden happier.

Carey looked at Lennox, who shrugged. Then Carey held a hand out. Camden jerked back when a flame appeared on his palm from out of nowhere.

"How did you do that?" he asked after making sure Carey wasn't moving to set the kitchen on fire.

Carey closed his palm, and the flame disappeared. "Lennox and I are phoenix shifters."

"Phoenix?" They were as rare as unicorns, and as sought after, although for different reasons. Where Toby and Sam could heal with their hands, phoenixes could create fire from thin air, like Carey had just done. It was an enormous advantage in battle, and they truly could mean that the pack would win against Springfield.

"Yep." Carey took his cup of coffee again. "As you probably know, we're rare, basically immortal in the sense that the only way we can die is by aging, and we can create fire."

"You're reckless nuts," Camden said. Phoenix shifters had a reputation. Because they always came back to life when they died violently, they tended to be afraid of very little. They threw themselves into fights and lived dangerously, which explained why the twins traveled from place to place to help people.

Carey laughed. "I guess I am. Lennox is much calmer, though."

Lennox hadn't yet said a word, and Camden wondered if he might be mute. Terrence hadn't said anything about that, and he wasn't about to ask. It wasn't his business, and as long as he and Carey could help, he didn't care, either.

"People are wary of you," Toby pointed out.

"They shouldn't be. We're okay people, I think."

"You like danger."

"We do jobs no one else wants to do because if they die, they stay dead. We don't. That doesn't mean we're bad people. We wouldn't be here to help you if we were."

"*Why* are you here? You don't know us. Why do you care about what the Springfield pack is doing? About my brother and me?"

"We're alone for a reason," Lennox said.

Camden almost dropped his mug in surprise.

"What do you mean?" Toby asked.

"Our family was decimated, taken. Our father died of a heart attack. Our mother poisoned herself. We were left alone because people were afraid of us. We decided to use that fear to help people. The ones who reach out to us for help might be afraid, or wary, but they need us, and in time, they usually realize we're normal people."

"I wouldn't call myself normal," Carey piped in. "Normal is boring."

Lennox rolled his eyes. "Of course. God help us if anyone considers you boring."

Carey waved his brother's words away. "What Lennox is trying to say is that we only have each other, and we've seen what fear and assholes can do. We're not going to allow the Springfield pack to take anyone away from this place, not when you guys don't want to go anywhere."

"And you think you'll be enough?" Toby asked. He was talking like an alpha mate, like someone who would help Camden guide the pack. It was a relief. Camden had been doing this for five years, and while he did have some help from Griffin and Leslie, it wasn't the same thing. They looked up to him to make the decisions, even when they helped him walk through the options. Toby would be different, though. He already was.

Carey arched a brow. "Well, we both have the power to set stuff on fire. That includes envoys, alphas, you get the drill.

We can do it at a distance, too. We don't need to be touching whatever we want to set on fire. With two of us, you can get rid of *armies*. The Springfield pack won't stand a chance against us."

"I'd like to avoid unnecessary deaths," Camden said. The last thing he wanted was to pass on the wrong side of things.

"We don't have to kill anyone. I might be weird, but I'm not an idiot. We're here to help, not to make things worse. We'll make sure the Springfield pack knows they shouldn't try anything with you, and we'll stay long enough to make it happen."

"How long?" Camden thought they did mean well, but this would be a moot point if the Springfield pack simply waited for the twins to leave to come back.

Carey shrugged. "No idea. We'll consult with you and make sure the pack is safe before we go anywhere, of course."

"What do you want in exchange for our protection?"

"That makes us sound like great people," Carey said, elbowing his brother in the side.

Lennox grunted, and he was the one who said, "Shelter and food until we find a job in town."

"Why would you want to find a job if you're going to leave?" Toby asked.

"We won't leave for a while. We need to keep you safe. It might take weeks or even months, and I don't like to sit on my ass and do nothing."

Camden cleared his throat. "We can do that. We can also probably pay you something for the protection you're offering."

"We don't want to get paid for that," Carey intervened. "We'll be honorary pack members while we're here, and we don't want to be treated differently. As Lennox said, we only need a place to stay, and if you could point us toward jobs, it'd be great. We have money to buy the stuff we need for now."

Camden nodded. "You can stay here for now. I'll ask the pack members if they have spare bedrooms unless you're okay staying here."

"We wouldn't want to inconvenience you. You probably want the house to yourselves."

Camden looked at Toby in question. Toby shrugged and nodded. Camden turned back to Carey. "We have enough free bedrooms. This is the house I grew up in, and I have a brother and a sister. There are five bedrooms, and Toby and I are only using one. You can pick the ones you want."

"Thank you."

An urgent knock on the door made Camden start. What was happening now? He hoped it was someone checking in because they'd noticed the twins, but when he opened the door and found Griffin there, he knew it was much worse than that from his expression. "What is it?"

"The envoy is back."

Toby bounced his knee. He was staring at the office door, waiting for Griffin to let the envoy in. He knew he shouldn't show this kind of weakness, no matter how he felt, but he couldn't help it. Was this it? Was this the last moments he spent with Camden? After this morning and everything that had happened since Toby had arrived in Rosewood, he never wanted to leave. He hadn't been sure he could ever have a home again after his parents' death, but he did, and he didn't want to lose everything again. He'd leave if he had to, to protect Sam, but he *really* wanted to stay. He'd never thought he'd think that, but here he was.

"Stop it."

Toby blinked at the sound of Lennox's voice. "What?"

"Your knee. I know you're nervous, but it's driving me

crazy, and it's going to show the envoy how anxious you are. You should try to stop bouncing it."

That was what Toby had been thinking, but he didn't like getting caught. "Sorry."

"Don't apologize. I'd be surprised if you weren't nervous. I understand. But the envoy is going to look for signs of weakness, and while being nervous isn't one, it's still a sign that something is wrong, that he's getting to you."

"You're right. Thank you."

Lennox nodded. "You're not going anywhere, and neither is your brother. Don't worry. Carey and I have your back."

Toby wanted to ask why, even though they'd already gone over that when they'd met earlier, but a knock on the door made him jump on his chair. Camden took his hand and smiled at him, then called out, "Come in."

The door opened, and Griffin stepped in. "Alpha Cook. The Springfield pack envoy."

"Let him in."

John Harris was smiling when he walked in. He looked around the room, his gaze pausing on Toby and his smirk widening, only to dim when he saw Lennox and Carey. Lennox was standing behind Toby's chair, but Carey had decided that was too stiff for him, and he was lounging in an extra chair on the other side of the desk. He was sitting sideways, with his legs dangling off one of the arms. He looked like he was relaxing rather than being in a tense meeting that would decide Toby and Sam's fate. He was checking his nails and didn't seem to have one care in the world, but Toby needed to trust him and Lennox. They were here, and they'd promised they'd help. He had to believe they would.

"I didn't expect you to want an audience for this," the envoy said. He didn't sit down like he had the day before.

"And I didn't expect you to come back until tomorrow," Camden answered. He sounded cold and like he wanted to strangle the envoy with his bare hands. He probably did. *Toby* did.

"My alpha didn't appreciate the way you're wasting time."

"We're not wasting time. I already told you my answer. Sam and Toby are both staying. That's all the answer you're ever going to get from me."

"That's a pity. This place is . . . picturesque. I can't imagine what it will look like once Alpha Wilson is done with you."

"Oh, why don't you keep your threats to yourself and fuck off?" Carey said. He sounded like he didn't have a care in the world, and he was grinning like a loon, something he seemed to do all the time. Toby had never known anyone who smiled that much.

The envoy jerked. "How dare you—" he stepped toward Carey, then thought better of it. "I have no idea who you are, but rest assured that my alpha will deal with you." He looked around the room. "With *all* of you. You could have kept one of them, Cook, but instead, you're sacrificing your pack and your husband in the name of doing the right thing."

"You say that like he's an idiot for respecting Toby and Sam's wishes," Carey said.

"The pack should come before them."

"And you shouldn't be an asshole, yet here we are. Lenny, why don't you show this guy why he and his alpha should stay away from Toby and Sam."

Toby's eyes widened. He had no idea how Carey managed to sound like he was talking about what he wanted to eat for dinner. Actually, he suspected Carey took his dinner more seriously than he was taking the envoy, and he could see how angry the envoy was at that.

"How dare you—" the envoy snapped.

Then his coat caught fire.

Toby jerked, and a hand clamped on his shoulder. He looked up to see Lennox holding him while staring at the envoy. His expression was the same as it had been before—still serious and uninterested—even though he'd just set a man on fire.

The envoy screamed and tried to take his coat off. Toby didn't want the man to die, even though he was trying to ruin his life, and he was relieved when the fire disappeared as suddenly as it had appeared.

The envoy snapped this head toward them. "How dare you." He growled, and Toby pressed his back against his chair when he realized the envoy was shifting.

Was he really going to shift into his wolf and attack Toby while Camden, Leslie, Griffin, and the twins were there? Even though he had nothing to do with the fire?

A wall of muscles and clothes made the world disappear. Lennox had stepped in front of Toby, and when the envoy shook his clothes off and jumped over the desk, Lennox caught him.

He grunted and threw the envoy back on the other side of the desk while Camden gathered Toby in his arms. Carey, Leslie, and Griffin wrestled the envoy to the floor, and Camden let go of Toby, rising to his feet and walking around the desk. He stood over the wolf, who was once again shifting to his human form.

"You are no longer welcome here, Harris. The next time you come, Carey and Lennox will take care of you, and you won't have the chance to walk away then. The same will happen to your alpha and any of your pack members if they come. Sam and Toby are Rosewood pack members, and that's not going to change unless *they* decide it should."

Toby couldn't see that happening, ever. He and Sam had found a home, a place where they belonged and where they didn't have to fear being attacked, manipulated, or abused. They were never going to leave.

"My alpha—" the envoy began.

Carey crouched next to his head and flicked his fingers, set-ting Harris' hair on fire. He ignored Harris' screams and said, "Your alpha is going to go up in smoke if I see him around. You heard Alpha Cook. You and your people aren't welcome here. I won't have a problem making a bonfire out of you." He flicked his fingers again, and the fire vanished.

Harris' face was red and sweaty, but from where he was, Toby could see he wasn't wounded. Carey had been very pre-cise, burning only the man's hair—and possibly, his dignity.

Camden sounded every bit like the alpha he was when he said, "Griffin, Leslie, please escort Mr. Harris outside and make sure he leaves pack territory." The *and that he doesn't come back* wasn't said out loud, but it was implied.

Toby turned his attention to Lennox, who was still stand-ing in front of him, protecting him. Toby was touched—Len-nox didn't even know him, and while the reason he and his brother were here was to protect Toby, Sam, and the pack, Toby had never expected that he would step in front of him the way he had.

Toby rose from his chair and stepped around Lennox, gasping when he saw the gashes in Lennox's arms. Harris had his claws out when he'd jumped over the desk, and he'd been aiming for Toby. If his pack couldn't have Toby, then no pack could, apparently, and Lennox had been wounded in his place.

"You're hurt," Toby said.

Lennox shrugged. "Just a few scratches."

Blood was dripping from Lennox's arms. "That looks more serious than a few scratches."

"I've had worse."

Toby could believe that considering the way Lennox was reacting. "Sit down."

"I don't need to sit down."

Toby arched a brow. "Maybe not, but you're too big for me

to heal you while you're standing. I don't want to hurt my neck trying."

"You don't have to heal me."

"Are you really saying no to my order?"

The corner of Lennox's lips twitched. "I hadn't realized it was an order. Pardon me, Alpha Mate." He sat in the chair Toby had vacated and held his arms out.

Toby winced at the sight. He'd seen worse, but the fact that Lennox was hurt because of him made him feel guilty, even though Lennox had volunteered. He grabbed a tissue from Camden's desk and tried to dry the blood as he worked so he could see more.

"No one has ever done this for me," Lennox murmured. He was staring at the wounds Toby was closing on his arms.

"I'll always heal you if you need it." Toby was surprised to realize it was true. He *would* always heal people if they needed it, including Lennox and Carey.

Maybe he was supposed to be a healer after all.

Camden had hoped things would go well, but they'd exceeded his expectations. He'd suspected Harris wouldn't take their no for an answer. He *hadn't* expected the man to shift and try to attack Toby. That didn't even make sense. Harris was there to take one of the brothers, so why would he try to kill Toby? It was weird to think that he might have let anger get the better of him. There was a reason he'd been chosen to come to Rosewood and make the Springfield's pack demands. An impulsive person wouldn't have been the right pick.

"There," Toby said.

Camden had given him and Lennox space when Toby had decided to heal the phoenix. Toby wasn't usually one to reach for people, and Camden had never seen him use his power. He'd thought Toby didn't want to be a healer, and maybe he didn't. He was good at it, though, there was no denying that.

"This was fun," Carey said as he flopped into his chair again.

Lennox grunted. "I wouldn't call it fun. Did you *have* to provoke him?"

"I didn't provoke him." Lennox scowled at Carey. Carey laughed. "Okay, maybe I provoked him a bit. But come on, Lenny. He's an asshole. He would have found a reason to attack even if I hadn't said anything. He *wanted* a fight after Camden told him he could fuck off."

"If I remember correctly, *you* were the one who told him to fuck off," Camden said.

Carey shrugged. "Maybe. We were all thinking it, though."

That much was true. The only reason Camden hadn't told the envoy what he thought of him and his pack was that he was the alpha. He couldn't be honest when he thought another alpha was being a dick, especially not in front of that alpha's envoy.

"Do you think it's over?" Toby asked. He sat back into the chair he'd occupied, his shoulders slumped. He looked tired. He probably *was* tired. All of them had stayed tense ever since Harris had first come to the pack, and even now that he was gone, it wasn't going to be easy to let go of the fear that he and his pack could appear at any moment and take Sam and Toby away.

"I suggest we have breakfast," Carey said. "I'm starving."

Lennox snorted. "Of course you are."

Camden could already tell those two—but especially Carey—were going to make his life harder. Carey wouldn't have a problem telling off people for being assholes over thinking Camden should have an heir. He'd ruffle feathers, but maybe that wasn't a bad thing. Camden kind of wished the twins would stay, and not just because the pack was safer with them there. He liked them, even though he had known them only a few hours.

"Why did you heal me?" Lennox asked quietly.

Toby was still cleaning his arms of the blood, and he looked nonplussed by the question. "Because you were hurt."

"Would it have made a difference if I hadn't been protecting you when I got hurt?"

"Of course not. I might still not be sure I want to be a healer, but I would never leave someone in pain if I could help them."

Lennox looked at Carey. Something passed between them, and they both nodded. Camden had no idea what that meant, but he was grateful when Lennox said, "We'll accept your offer of staying here with you and your husband, Alpha Cook. We want to make sure no one else is going to come to try getting Sam and Toby. No one has any right over them and their lives except them, and we'll make sure they're not forced into anything they don't want."

Camden wasn't sure why this was so important for the twins, but the *why* didn't matter. He was gaining two strong fighters, even if they couldn't beat a fly. Their fire powers were enough for them to be extremely valuable to any pack or group of shifters, and he wasn't going to look a gift horse in the mouth. "Thank you. You're welcome to stay for as long as you want."

"We appreciate the offer," Lennox said.

From what Camden knew, they'd both been drifting for a while, bouncing from pack to pack. Maybe they felt it was time to stop, or maybe they'd eventually leave. Whatever they decided, Camden was going to make sure they felt welcome with the pack.

Breakfast was weird, to say the least. Camden had barely gotten used to cooking for two after five years preparing food only for himself, and now he had to add another two people. Toby had ordered Lennox to sit down and rest, even though Lennox had protested, but Carey was surprisingly helpful, and he took over the preparation of the pancakes while Camden focused on the eggs and bacon.

"I think we're going to like living here," Carey said. He kept sneaking a hand toward the plate where Camden put the bacon that was ready and stealing pieces.

Camden wasn't sure how Carey could be this comfortable. He'd just arrived. He barely knew Camden. Yet he was behaving as if he'd lived there for months, as if he considered Camden a friend. It wasn't a bad thing, but Camden wasn't used to it. The only two people who didn't treat him differently after he'd become alpha were Frederic and Reece. Bryson also didn't care much, but he was Camden's brother, so it was different. But the rest of the pack was respectful, sometimes too much so. It was weird, after some of them had yelled at Camden when he was a kid because he kept stealing the strawberries from their vegetable gardens.

"You think so?" he asked Carey. When Carey reached for another strip of bacon, Camden took a risk and gently tapped his wrist with the wooden spoon he was using to mix the eggs in the pan.

Carey snatched his hand away and glared, but that soon dissolved into a smile. "Yeah. I mean, look at you, already putting me in my place for stealing bacon."

"There won't be any left if I allow you to eat it all before we even sit at the table."

"You're right, but I love bacon." He pouted. "Seriously, though. You look like a nice guy. A good alpha. You could have taken the easy way out and handed off your mate's brother, but you didn't."

"Toby would never have forgiven me for that."

"Maybe, but you don't need him, do you? I mean, yeah, he's your soul mate, and that shit doesn't happen every day, but I'm pretty sure most of the pack would rather see you with a lady. You're the alpha. You need someone to take your place when you can't do your job anymore. Come on. The easiest way for you to deal with everything would have been to hand off one of them. The other would have been pissed, but you could have justified this by pointing out you were protecting the entire pack. It wouldn't have been a lie."

"But I wouldn't have been able to live with myself."

Carey pointed his spatula at Camden. "And *that's* why you're a good guy. You want people to be free and happy, and you're going to do what you can for that to happen. You would have done this even if Toby hadn't been your mate."

"I would have, yes." It was a no brainer, and Camden didn't understand why Carey was making a big deal out of it.

Two arms slipped around Camden's waist from behind. He smiled and leaned back against Toby. "Hey. You're done mothering Lennox?"

Camden couldn't see Toby, but he could hear the scowl in his voice. "I wasn't mothering him, just making sure he was okay, and he is."

"Thanks for healing him," Carey said. "You didn't have to."

Toby shrugged. "Of course I did. He was hurt, and I have the ability to heal. I couldn't ignore his pain."

Carey grinned as if Toby had proved his point. "You both are good people."

"It's basic human decency," Toby pointed out.

"For you, maybe. But Lennox and I have been around, and trust me, we've seen things that would horrify you, people behaving like assholes because they could, and they had the power to do it. This is a nice place because Camden is a good alpha. He treats people with respect even though he's their alpha. Think about it. If he'd been an asshole and he'd decided to keep you and Sam because you could be useful, what would have stopped one of the pack members from grabbing one of you and handing you to the Springfield pack? Nothing.

The pack didn't do it because they respect him and his leadership. And because they love him."

Camden had never thought about it that way, and it made him feel all squirmy and humbled. He'd never been sure he was doing a good job as his father's heir, but maybe he was.

CHAPTER SEVEN

This was the life Toby had always wanted and hadn't let himself hope he could have. He'd gone from being a captive to having his brother back, a husband, a home, friends. Sometimes he had a hard time wrapping his mind around it, but he hoped that time would help him stop feeling like he might lose all of this with the flick of a finger.

"Are you sure they won't mind?" Lennox asked, his voice barely more than a whisper as he leaned close to Toby. For some reason, he didn't seem to mind talking to Toby, even though he was mostly quiet with everyone else.

Toby didn't mind. It made him feel special. He wanted Lennox to have a friend, and if he was the only one Lennox felt comfortable with, that was okay.

Toby patted Lennox's arm. "Of course they won't mind. They wouldn't have invited you otherwise."

Lennox and Carey had been with the pack one week, and they were still settling in. Everyone was curious about them, though, and when Frederic and Sam had decided to host a barbecue, they'd invited the twins along with Camden and Toby. Reece and Sage would be there too, but that was it. No one wanted to overwhelm the twins, although Carey probably wouldn't mind. He loved being with people, and he often walked up to them and started chatting. He'd already gotten all of Toby's life story out of Toby, and Toby wasn't one for talking a lot.

"Who's going to be there?"

"Just us, my brother and his mate, and a couple of close

friends. That's it. No one expects you to make conversation. You can stay in your corner and glower at anyone coming close. We don't get offended."

Lennox glared, but Toby could tell he wasn't angry by the slight curl of his lips. "I don't stand in corners glowering."

"You *so* do, Lennox. But that's okay. No one here is going to bug you, I promise. We told them you're not a talker, and I'm pretty sure they're going to be busy with Carey anyway. He talks enough for both of you." And then some. He probably talked enough for four people. "Both my brother and Sage are the quiet type, like you. You can sit with them."

When they got to Sam's house, he, Frederic, Sage, and Reece were in the backyard getting the grill ready and talking. The air was cold, but it felt good to be outside. Toby still wasn't used to being able to do it any time he wanted. After four years locked in a house, he *needed* to spend time outside, and he'd dressed accordingly.

"Oh, who's the cutie?" Carey asked before they could even get to the small group of men.

Toby rolled his eyes. "There you go again. Who do you mean?"

"The one with the round ass and the long hair."

"That's Sage." Toby hesitated. As far as he knew, Sage and Reece weren't together, even though he didn't understand why. "He and Reece have something going on," he said. He wasn't sure that was the right word, but it was better than not saying anything.

"Aww, you mean he's taken, too?"

"Not exactly. I don't think he and Reece are officially together, but I know they're close, and I'm pretty sure Reece is in love with Sage, or at the very least that he likes him."

"But they're not together."

"You're going to have to ask them if you want to be sure of that."

"I can deal with some competition."

"I'm sure you can. But they care about each other. I don't know why they're not a couple, but I don't want either of them to get hurt." Toby wasn't exactly friends with them, but Sam was, and even though he didn't know them well, Toby didn't want Carey to play with anyone's emotions. Things would be different if he were serious about Sage, but until he got to know Sage, there was no way to be sure he would be.

"I'll make sure he doesn't make an ass out of himself," Lennox said. "I've been doing that since we were born."

"Only because you're a few minutes older than me," Carey said. He never seemed to get angry. Even when he'd faced the envoy, he'd sounded carefree, but not angry.

"Just keep your hands to yourself."

"I'm not an asshole, Lenny. You know that. I won't do anything the cutie doesn't want."

"What about the other one? Don't get us kicked out, Carey."

"Nobody will kick you out," Toby tried to reassure them. "As long as you behave the right way, you're welcome here."

"Even with Carey being an overexcited puppy?"

Toby had to smile at that. "Even with him. I like having him around. He colors my days." That was true. Being around Carey was never dull, and Toby would love it if the twins decided to stay indefinitely. He wasn't going to mention that, though, not yet, not until they spent more time here.

Carey made a beeline for Sage once they were close enough. He never let anything stop him, and Reece's glare wasn't any different. Carey stopped in front of Sage and smiled at him, leaning closer. "Hey, beautiful."

Sage blinked at him. "Hello."

Toby frowned when Carey leaned even closer, almost pushing his nose against Sage's neck. It reminded Toby of what he'd done when he'd first met Camden, and he held his breath, wondering if that was what was happening.

Reece took Sage's arm and pulled him back. "What the fuck are you doing?" he snapped.

Carey smiled at Reece. "I'm smelling my mate. What about you?"

Reece paled and dropped Sage's arm. Toby didn't think he was wrong when he thought that Sage looked hurt that he did. "He's your mate?" Reece asked, his voice pained.

Carey nodded once. "He is."

Reece nodded and stepped away. "Sorry."

Sage *definitely* looked pained now. He stared at Reece as Reece retreated, and Toby wanted to go to him and soothe him. He had no idea what was going on, and he knew he should probably stay out of it, but Sage was his friend.

"He's going to ruin everything," Lennox bemoaned.

"He just met his mate. Aren't you happy?" Maybe he wasn't, because he and Carey were supposed to leave eventually.

"Of course I'm happy for him. I want him to have what you and Camden have. But we're new here, and the last thing we need is for him to create trouble."

"He hasn't done anything."

"Maybe not, but you saw what happened. I don't know if you were right and if your friends were together, but even if they weren't, they're both bothered by what's happening, and knowing Carey, he's going to try to bowl through everything to get what he wants."

"As long as he doesn't hurt Sage, I don't see how it's our business."

"Maybe not, but that doesn't mean I'm not worried." Lennox left Toby to grab a beer from the cooler by the grill.

Toby wasn't sure what to do with himself. Lennox wasn't wrong when he said this was a delicate situation. There was obviously something between Sage and Reece, and having

Carey there, him being Sage's mate, wasn't going to make things easier.

"They'll be fine," Camden said as he wrapped an arm around Toby's shoulders.

"I hope so."

"We'll keep an eye on them, make sure no one does something they'll regret. They have to solve this on their own, though."

"Do you think Reece will end up alone?"

"Maybe. It depends on Sage, doesn't it? Carey might be his mate, but that doesn't mean they have to be together. Sage is going to have to weigh his options and make the decision. He and Reece have been poking at each other for a while now. Maybe this situation is going to give Reece the guts, or whatever else he needed, to talk to Sage."

"There has to be a reason they're not together."

"Maybe there is, or maybe they're both too cautious. Again, we don't know, and it's none of our business." He kissed Toby's forehead. "Come on. Let's go see if we can help Frederic."

He was right. Toby could heal a lot of things, but he couldn't do anything about this. He wished he could, though. He wanted his friends to be happy, as happy as he was.

But they were going to have to find their own paths to that happiness.

You may also enjoy the following from eXtasy Books Inc:

Gabriel
Catherine Lievens

Excerpt

Gabriel's eyes felt so dry, he was seriously thinking about gouging them. Maybe he could throw them in the sink and hydrate them or something. Anything would feel better than the way he was feeling now.

"Did you take the plate of the van that hit you?" Oliver asked from the open door.

Gabriel blinked. "What?"

"You look like shit, and you didn't come to help with dinner."

"Shit." Gabriel checked the time, and sure enough, it was almost eleven PM. "I'm sorry. I was checking the budget, and—"

Oliver raised a hand. "It's fine. We made do without you, don't worry."

"You should have come get me."

"Luke and I both knew you were working, and that you're probably exhausted. What time did you leave the library today?"

"Uh, six, I think? It was story time this afternoon, and the kids always leave a bit of a mess."

"So you went home, freshened up, and came here. Did you even eat dinner?"

"I had a sandwich. You don't have to worry about me, Ollie. I'm an adult." Hell, Gabriel would hit thirty this year. He mostly still felt like the terrified kid who'd arrived in Gillham almost thirteen years ago, even though he wasn't anymore.

"I know I don't have to. Doesn't mean I'm not going to, and I'm not the only one. What does Alice think of your timetable?"

"She's not happy." Oliver was going to find out anyway. He and Alice were friends. The five of them—Gabriel, Alice, Oliver, Maddox, and Lilah. They'd spent the last years of their teenage period living in the same house, and they were close. Some of them more than others, but that didn't change the fact that they all stuck their noses in each other's business.

"She tried to get you to quit again?"

"Not yet, but she's going to." Gabriel saved the sheet he'd been working on and turned the computer off. The budget could wait until tomorrow.

"Of course she is, and she's not wrong. I don't get why you don't want Kam to pay for her education like he did with the rest of us."

"She's my responsibility." And nothing was going to change that. "How are things in the kitchen? Is there something I can help you with?"

"Nah. We cleaned up and locked the doors. We can go home."

Gabriel smiled. "You need a ride?" Oliver always did. He owned a bike, but he knew Gabriel didn't like seeing him on that death trap, so he didn't usually use it when he volunteered at the shelter.

Oliver grinned. "Yeah, but I'm driving. You look like you're going to go headfirst into a ditch because you'll fall asleep at the wheel."

"You don't have to do that." Even though it was true that Gabriel felt like he might fall asleep any second."

"I know. I'll sleep on your couch, yeah? That way Alice and I can catch up tomorrow morning. You can drive me back to town when you go to work."

Gabriel knew it was more for his benefit than because Ollie wanted to catch up with Alice, but he was grateful. He always felt like he didn't have enough time to spend with his friends. He was always busy with work, and when he wasn't, he was sleeping.

"Come on, Gabe. Let's go home. I'm sure Alice left you dinner."

"I'm not sharing," Gabriel grumbled even though they both knew he would. Hell, Oliver had probably called Alice to let her know he was coming. She'd had the time to cook for three rather than two.

"You're a mean, mean man."

They met Luke at the back door and left together. Gabriel was the one in charge of locking up, so he did that while Oliver and Luke talked. Then Luke waved goodbye and headed home to his mate while Gabriel trudged to his car. He was grateful Oliver had volunteered to drive. Right now, sleeping in the shelter's parking lot sounded good, and Gabriel wasn't sure he'd be able to stay awake until they were home. He was going to try, of course—he didn't want Oliver to have to be on his own for the ride, even though the house was only ten minutes away. It would be a lousy way to thank him.

"You know you can call me if you need anything," Oliver said once they were in the car.

"I know."

"Including money."

"I'm not asking you for a loan. I don't need a loan. I like both my jobs."

"I realize that. I'm just saying that if you finally stopped being pigheaded and accepted Kam's help like we all did, you could quit your job at the shelter but stay on as a volunteer.

You wouldn't have to think about budgets and locking up and all that stuff. You'd be free to focus on the helping people part."

Gabriel wanted that so very much, but he couldn't have it. Alice was his family, his sister in all but in blood, and he was supposed to take care of her and provide for her. The fact that she was twenty-six didn't change that, and neither did knowing that the pack could afford to send her to college ten times over. It was a question of principles, no matter how stupid it sounded right now and how much Gabriel wanted to give in.

"You're not going to do it, are you?" Oliver asked. He sounded resigned. He knew Gabriel well enough to know his answer already.

"I can't."

"Whatever, man. You totally can, but I'm not going to push. God knows that's not going to help. You're as stubborn as a mule. You're sure you're a skunk shifter?"

Gabriel lightly slapped Oliver's arm. "Shut it."

"You need time off, Gabe. You can't continue like this. You're going to collapse, and no one here wants that, least of all you. Who's gonna work your two jobs if you're not able to do it?"

"Can we not talk about this?"

Oliver sighed. "Yeah. It's not like I'm gonna change your mind anyway."

"I wish I could."

"Me too. I mean, I get why you're doing it, why you think that way. I do. I might not have been through what you and Alice went through, but my parents kicked me out, too. I didn't spend as long on the streets as you guys, but that doesn't mean I don't feel like I owe the pack everything I have now. I wouldn't have the shop without Kam. I wouldn't have anything. Hell, I'd probably be dead, and I have no idea how I can ever pay Kameron back. But maybe I don't have to pay him back, not in money."

"Ollie—" Gabriel knew what his friend was getting at, but

they'd already been over this, and they didn't think the same way.

"You're useful to the pack and the town. You work at the library. You work at the shelter. That's more than enough for Kam, and you know it. He's paid for all us kids' college if we wanted to go. He invested in my bike shop. In return, he expects me to be a good pack member and to help when he needs me. I know he's a good guy and that he's not going to force me to do something I don't want to do or to hold this over my head forever."

"Come on, Ollie. You said we could stop talking about it."

"We will. I just want to say one more thing."

Gabriel sighed. "I'm listening."

"Taking his money without paying it back wouldn't be taking advantage of him or the pack. Kameron puts that money aside for this purpose. He wants to take care of us because he's a good alpha, and we're his pack members. That's literally his job, and you're not allowing him to do that. You're even paying him rent when all of us other pack members live rent-free in whatever house we chose. You need to stop being a martyr and start living a little, and that's not going to happen if you spend more than twelve hours working every day."

Gabriel couldn't deny anything Oliver had said. He was right, and Kameron had tried to make Gabriel see that more than once. Gabriel didn't seem to be able to let go of the feeling that he owed Kameron this and much more, though—of the feeling that if he didn't pay what he owed back, Kameron was going to kick him and Alice out, and they'd be once again alone in the world.

About the Author

Catherine lives in Italy, country of good food and hot men. She used to write fantasy as a child, but it was reading her first gay erotic romance novel that made her realize that that was what she really wanted to write.

After graduating from college in English language and translation, she divides her day between writing, reading, taking care of her son and reading some more.

You can find her on Facebook and Twitter or on her website: authorcatherinelievens.wordpress.com

Email: lievens.catherine@gmail.com

Newsletter: http://eepurl.com/c-uvKn

www.ingramcontent.com/pod-product-compliance
Lightning Source LLC
Chambersburg PA
CBHW060629130626
46555CB00002B/729